Vasquez Private Eye

A Fable of Murder and the Unknown Truth

Evil is like death; the truth lies beyond what the mortal eye can see, and only those who have been consumed by it can know what dreadful secrets hide under its disguise.

Edward Bardes

Vasquez Private Eye

By Edward Bardes

Johnson Vasquez is a policeman with a highly troubled past. He survived a plane crash, and in the six years following the disaster, his friends have undergone surreal changes. What he doesn't realize is that as he attempts to move forward, the crash will come back to haunt him.

Johnson and his partner, Zelda Thomson, are working to unravel a series of court cases gone horribly awry. As the investigation is conducted, a cryptic note comes into Johnson's possession. In little more than an hour, a murderer strikes.

What started as a normal day at work suddenly spirals into one of the biggest murder mysteries in the state. Johnson must find the clues and stop the killer. But nothing could prepare him for the truth, the whole truth, and nothing but the truth, so help him God.

Printed in the United States of America
ISBN 978-1-64133-821-9 (sc)
ISBN 978-1-64133-822-6 (e)
ISBN 978-1-64133-823-3 (hc)

This book is printed on acid-free paper.

Because of the dynamic nature of the Internet, any web addresses or links contained in this book may have changed since publication and may no longer be valid. The views expressed in this work are solely those of the author and do not necessarily reflect the views of the publisher, and the publisher hereby disclaims any responsibility for them.

2024.04.29

BlueInk Media Solutions
1111B S Governors Ave
STE 7582 Dover,
DE 19904

www.blueinkmediasolutions.com

CONTENTS

Chapter I: How It Began 1

Chapter II: Landenberg 6

Chapter III: Johnson's Story 11

Chapter IV: The Journey 16

Chapter V: Murder #1 21

Chapter VI: Discussion 26

Chapter VII: Alex's Story 32

Chapter VIII: Wainwright Law 37

Chapter IX: Murder #2 43

Chapter X: Cops Compete 48

Chapter XI: Richard's Story 53

Chapter XII: Trial of Error 58

Chapter XIII: Zachary Venshlin 64

Chapter XIV: Murder #3 69

Chapter XV: Shannon's Story 74

Chapter XVI: Train of Thought 79

Chapter XVII: The Backstab 84

Chapter XVIII: The Alliance 89

Chapter XIX: Zelda's Story 95

Chapter XX: The Involvement 100

Chapter XXI: Murder #4 105

Chapter XXII: Numb Fingers 110

Chapter XXIII: The Loss.. 115

Chapter XXIV: The Discovery 120

Chapter XXV: The Revelation... 125

Chapter XXVI: The Confrontation.. 131

Chapter XXVII: The Aftermath 136

Chapter XXVIII: Last Will and Testament 142

Chapter XXIX: The Killer's Story.. 147

Chapter XXX: The Endgame 152

Dedicated to Lyndsay Collins, my teacher.
– E. B.

Vasquez Private Eye

CHAPTER I

How It Began

Everyone has had a day they wish never to go through twice, but not me. One might swear by their life never to let it happen to them twice, but I would let it happen again if it came back to me. I live for adventure. I want to live a life full of excitement, danger, and unpredictability. I want a life I can live to the fullest, which is why I've decided to walk my father's footprints and become a police detective. You'd be surprised at what a life that can be, especially in my shoes.

My father, Daniel Jack Vasquez, has worked as a police detective for twenty-three years. He has cracked some of the town's toughest cases and is known for finding evidence others have overlooked. His job as a detective is actually how he met my mother, Martha Ida Laverne Faulkner.

It's a long story, actually. He had caught a man who killed his brother for sleeping with his wife. At the trial, he and my mother testified separately as witnesses. After the trial, the two of them started spending time together. Eventually, they got married, bought a condo, and had two kids, me and my brother Terrence.

My mother works as a chemistry teacher at the local university. She also works in the forensics laboratories, running tests on DNA, fingerprints, and other amazing stuff. One of her old students is a friend of mine, Shannon Thomson.

Shannon works as a forensic chemist and has been a bit of a weakling at times. Mom has served as a role model for her, and Terrence has helped her through tough times. Even so, she does tend to be very emotional.

Shannon's sister, Zelda, is also a police detective. She and I are partners in the police force, and she has shown herself to be a vital aid for me; she is a brilliant detective like my dad, and she is by my side when the chips are down.

Shannon's boyfriend, Richard Ralston, is a very ardent baseball player and is aspiring to be in the big leagues. He is an especially skilled pitcher. He has a younger brother, Patrick, who works at an insurance company and has come close to death himself. There's a murder trial coming up soon (from when I start telling the story), and Patrick would be a witness.

And then there's Alex Andrews. He has been a close friend of mine for a while. By day, he is a comical prank store owner. He's known for telling jokes, and I've learned a few as well. By night, he is a hard-willed bounty hunter with the alias Brandon Chide. He has proven very useful in setting traps for catching suspects. Trust me, they help.

My everyday activities revolve around police work with my dad. He is quite the cop if you ask me. Every day, Zelda and I patrol the streets in a squad car, and during the evenings, my dad and I work on cracking cases.

My dreams of being on the police team had started when I was only ten years old. My friends and I were playing together outside our school. Alex, Richard, Shannon, and Zelda played a "tug-of-war" prank. They stood on opposite sides of the street and pretended to play tug-of-war with an invisible rope. Patrick and I were playing basketball, and Terrence was at the swing set.

Alex, Richard, Shannon, and Zelda had fun watching frustrated drivers slow down and yell at them to take the game someplace else. Then we heard police sirens headed toward us. They exchanged panicked glances, thinking one of the victims called the police and told them about what they did.

We all ran straight for the school. Shannon and Zelda were on the other side of the street from the school, and as they were crossing the street, Shannon tripped over the curb. She picked herself up and ran straight towards the building without hesitation.

At that moment, a blue Hummer blared down the street towards us, followed by about six or seven police cruisers. The Hummer swerved, barely missing Shannon, and smacked into a tree. We all watched as ten officers jumped out of the cruisers, grabbed the driver from the wreck, clapped him in handcuffs, put him in a squad car, and drove off.

I went over to check on Shannon, who was still shaken from almost being killed. She was sprawled in the middle of the road, shuddering like a massage chair. Richard and I helped her up, but she was unable to stand. And so, we both held her up and walked her into the school lobby and laid her down on a bench.

That was when Terrence came over to see what had happened. "What happened here?"

"My sister almost got hit by a car," Zelda answered.

"Terrence, go get Mom and Dad," I instructed.

He and Patrick got on their bikes and headed back to the condo, which was just across the highway from the school.

Richard and Alex went to get some water for Shannon while Zelda and I looked after her.

About an hour after Patrick and Terrence left, Mom and Dad arrived, as well as Shannon and Zelda's parents.

Mrs. Thomson knelt down next to the bench where her daughter was laying. "Are you okay, Shannon?"

Her whimpering tempered her words to watery tears.

Richard and Alex came back with the water. She sipped in small swallows, taking shaky breaths in between each gulp.

It was about an hour before she managed to calm down enough to be escorted to my and Terrence's place for the night and get herself together.

Mom showed everyone into the condo. "Alright kids, make yourselves at home. Just sit Shannon down on the couch, and we'll get dinner ready."

Dad and I helped Shannon inside the apartment while Richard and Terrence helped out Mom in making dinner. Alex and Zelda went to the living room to watch TV, where a news report was showing the scene we had witnessed that afternoon.

"So, what are we having for dinner?" I asked Terrence.

"Mackerel and rice," he replied disgustedly as he went to the fridge to make himself a sandwich.

Shannon was asleep in the living room when the meal was brought to the table. The smell was enough to bring the whole city to our condo. She got herself up and came over to the table with the rest of us.

As we were eating dinner, I started wondering what it would be like to be on the police team. I mentioned this to Dad the next day. He promised to teach me everything he could, and Mom decided to help where she could, too.

And that's how it all started.

Being the thrill seeker that I am, working in an office is something I've never been fond of. Getting out of bed early in the morning, sitting in an office for eight hours a weekday, working at a computer and doing paperwork for a living; the ultimate mediocre experience one could possibly imagine. Not how one should spend his living years.

Strange as it may seem, that's actually where my story begins; more specifically, a law firm.

A man named William York had been charged with murdering his father, Scott, and trying to kill Patrick, who had narrowly escaped with his life. The trial would be underway in a few months, and I wanted to talk with the defense attorney.

I was at the diner having breakfast with my friends and parents. We were all in good spirits and were looking forward to the day ahead.

"So, did you sleep well last night, Professor Vasquez?" Shannon asked her former chemistry teacher.

"Yes, I did. Thank you," Mom responded to her former student. "What's new with you, Richard?"

"I got a new glove last week." He stood up to show the people at the table.

"Very nice," Zelda admired.

Alex was telling Dad a joke. I didn't hear what it was, but it made Dad laugh so hard I thought he would choke.

After breakfast, we all went our separate ways. Mom and Shannon went to the bus stop; Alex and Richard headed for the subway; and Zelda, Dad, and I drove our cruisers, Zelda and me together and Dad on his own.

As we drove off, Zelda and I began talking.

"So, what did you have planned for today, Johnson?"

"I've got a meeting with an attorney. What about you?"

"I'm still having a hard time with these mishaps I've been working with for the past month."

"Hm. Well, you know Patrick is taking part in the trial that's coming up."

"Yeah. I just hope nothing bad happens."

"Well, I was going to meet with the defense attorney today to hopefully shed light on these mysterious events."

Rumors have been spreading about court cases in the state that have ended with defendants being acquitted of all the charges pressed against them despite being truly guilty of them. Some believed that the trials were being rigged either by heavy corruption or saboteur intervention. No one has yet confirmed what exactly was causing this, but the mistrials have shaken the justice system to its core. Crime rates have reached an all-time high, and people have formed rallies protesting various aspects of the justice system.

"Maybe my dad can help," I offered.

"I've already asked him; he also seems to be having a lot of difficulty with this."

"Strange…" I thought.

I navigated Zelda through the heavily congested streets of downtown to the law firm where I would be meeting with the attorney. Even though Patrick was a prosecuting witness for the trial, I decided to meet with the defense attorney, Harold Satchel, since the DA, Gary McCrery, wasn't available to talk to.

As we approached the law firm, I took a glance in the side-view mirror and ran a comb through my hair.

Zelda pulled up to the curb, and I stepped out of the cruiser and straightened my tie before I headed through the glass doors at the entrance to the firm.

CHAPTER II

Landenberg

I climbed up the entrance's brick staircase and pushed on the door's brass rail. The inside looked like the inside of a luxury hotel lobby. The walls and ceiling were white with steel arches holding the roof up. The floor was black tile with gold trim, and large windows filled the expansive space with light.

I made my way to the front desk to ask them where to find the attorney. I was directed to the fifth floor in the west wing of the building, with the office number as 529.

The elevators stood just across the hall from the desk, but I took the stairs.

I was able to find the office with great facility.

Harold Satchel was waiting for me at his office. His pleasant face and blue eyes towered six feet up. He smoothed his dark yellow hair, straightened his tie, and gestured for me to come in. I shook his hand and stepped into his office.

"Hello, Johnson. I'm glad you were able to make it here today," Harold greeted me with a calm voice.

I pulled up a chair and sat down in front of his desk. "So, how are you today?"

"Quite well, thank you." He seated himself on his side of the desk opposite me.

Now, I couldn't imagine doing the mind-numbing work of a lawyer, but they deserve some recognition. They can make interesting things happen in the courtroom if they put forth enough effort, especially Harold Paul Wesley Satchel. He is one of the most famous attorneys in the state.

Now, don't get me wrong, I can think up witty things to say, but the only problem is that they never make it to my voice when I'm standing in front of several people. Terrence was the skilled talker in the family, not me.

As I sat at the desk and was getting ready to start the meeting, another attorney came into the office.

"Harold, can I please speak to you for a moment?"

"I'm busy right now; I'll talk to you later."

"It's important."

"How important is it?"

"I need to talk about it right now."

"Fine, I'm coming." He stood up and followed the man outside his office.

Twenty minutes went by. I waited in the office with bored impatience as the two men talked outside. As I waited, I took out my notepad and looked over a list I made of all the possible causes for the botched cases.

There were numerous theories circulating throughout the press, which ranged from swayed judges to overly careless prosecutors.

The one I had come back to again and again was the exclusionary rule.

Harold returned and we began our discussion.

"So, what did he want to tell you?"

"He said that I would be meeting with another attorney tomorrow."

"Who is he?"

"His name is Zachary Venshlin. He was hired here just yesterday, and I've been chosen to help him with his first week at the firm."

"I see. Was that him who just came in here?"

"No, that was my partner."

"Oh, okay. So, where were we?"

"We were getting ready to discuss the bad trials."

"Right. So, we don't have very many clues about who is doing all this, if this is a deliberate operation. I was hoping we could take a look at the past trials to see what, if anything, they have in common."

"So, is there a particular reason you chose to talk to me about this?"

"My friend's brother will be involved in the upcoming trial, and since you would be serving as the defense attorney and have an extraordinary understanding of the law, I thought I'd ask you about how someone might be able to carry out such an operation."

"I see. Do you have any information about the trials? If not, I could help you."

"That's another reason I wanted to talk to you. It seems some of the mistrials had you playing a major role."

"Yes, I have noticed that."

Satchel reached for the file cabinet under the desk and opened the lowest drawer. He walked his fingers through the large stack of folders and pulled one of them out and placed it on his desk.

"So, do you know who it was that first suspected a... sabotage operation with these trials?"

"That was one of several rumors that have been going around town."

"Is there evidence that would support such a claim?"

"Well, most of the trials may have reached an erroneous verdict by the exclusionary rule."

"Why would you say that?"

"Think about it. If you find something that screams out 'guilty,' and then you find that it was obtained illegally, the courts just say 'nope, can't use it' and they throw it out. What that does is destroy evidence, and that would ultimately allow a truly guilty wrongdoer to be acquitted."

"I see. There's also a possibility of a dissenting opinion which manages to obtain enough advocates."

"I have doubts about thirteen cases in a four-year time span all falling victim to that; after all, it's an extreme rarity for two trials to be identical."

"There are very few ways for a truly guilty defendant to be acquitted of all charges."

"I'm not sure if there's a more probable cause than a refusal to see blatant evidence because of warrant limitations."

"So, do you know if there is a mastermind behind all of these occurrences?"

"It seems very likely that that might be the case. Maybe if we look at all the cases that went wrong, we might have an answer to that question."

"Very well, then." Satchel reached into his file cabinet and pulled out the lowest drawer.

He found a folder filled with numerous papers, which he set down and opened on his desk.

I repositioned myself in my seat. "Did you take notes of each one already?"

"Yes, I did."

I was relieved. "At least we won't have to be here too long reading these documents."

"Right." He removed a stapled packet from the top.

"So, what have you found out about the cases?"

"Well, a few of them I was involved in personally, so I already have a few answers."

"Hm." I wasn't sure if that was beneficial or suspicious. "So, tell me about the cases you were involved in."

"The cases I was in were about drug-related crimes and robberies. I knew the people I was defending were guilty, so I was only trying to extenuate those clients. But surprisingly, all of those cases involved missing evidence which would have incriminated them. My clients then asked for me to get a 'not guilty' verdict for them. To my further surprise, I succeeded."

"Interesting. So, what were the other trials about?"

"The other court cases varied. At first, they were about civil cases such as parking violations and vandalism. But they soon started to deal with assault and other felonies; the most recent case was a kidnapping plot. In all cases, key evidence was missing or key people from the prosecution had to call in sick, and their replacements weren't anywhere near as skilled as those they were replacing."

"Hmm... I think there really is a saboteur on the loose if all of that were able to happen."

"So it would seem. They would all have to have one person in common in order for the allegation to be plausible."

"Maybe not. Maybe the outcomes are being decided by outside intervention."

"How do you believe that?"

"Maybe the judge is being tricked into favoring the defense instead of being bipartisan."

"It's doing no good to speculate. We need evidence to say what's happening and why."

"Yeah. And more importantly, we need to be able to identify a possible suspect for this."

"As far as I've seen, there's hardly anything that these cases have in common, so if someone is deliberating some kind of action, their involvement in each of them thus far seems to be undetermined."

It was then that the phone rang.

"Hello, thank you for calling Landenberg Criminal Law Firm. This is Harold Satchel speaking, how can I help you? ... Ah, hello, William. ... Well, I'm in the middle of a meeting right now. ... I'm being interviewed by a policeman right now. ... Calm down, calm down. ... Okay, I'll be on my way down there shortly."

"Who was that?"

"That was my client, William York."

"So, what did he want?"

"He's being interrogated by the police, and he's asking for me to be there."

"I've been meaning to talk to him as well; do you think I could talk with him after the interrogation?"

"What did you want to talk about?"

"I wanted to gain some insight about how a court case would be carried out; I heard he was involved in some other mischief before this."

"I'll ask him when the interrogation is finished."

"Very well, then." He put the folder on his desk back into its original spot in the cabinet and opened the drawer that stood directly above it.

He gathered all the files he needed and put them in a neat stack. He put the files in his briefcase, and we prepared to leave for the police station.

Chapter III

Johnson's Story

As great a cop as I am, I do have an Achilles heel: an extreme belief in Murphy's Law. I always think that pursuing dreams will end badly and won't allow any kind of recovery to try an alternative route.

I've been like that after I almost died in a plane crash.

When I was 20, my family and I were on a trip to Black Mesa in Oklahoma during Spring Break. My uncle and cousins lived in Denver and were joining us on our trip.

The date was March 29th, and our vacation was drawing to a close. We had had a fun time and were ready to go home. After dropping our cousins off at their house, we packed our bags and headed for the airport.

I rarely use airplanes for transportation because of how tall I am. Inside of an MD-80, I have to look down at the floor to avoid touching my head on the ceiling. On a 767, there's enough clearance for me to look straight ahead while walking.

Our scheduled flight was Firebird Airlines Flight 934 from Denver, Colorado to Cincinnati, Ohio. We were supposed to leave at 6:30 PM Mountain Time, but before we reached the plane, a severe thunderstorm came by, and we were forced to wait at the airport for an hour.

As soon as the storm cleared, we were finally allowed to board our flight to head home. I think everyone was bored waiting to get on.

Mom and I were seated adjacent to the left aisle of the plane, and Dad and Terrence were adjacent to the right. All of us were seated in the fifth row.

But five minutes after we were cleared to board, there was another setback.

The first officer was late getting to his post, so we got held up for a further 15 minutes. Terrence had suggested that we should book flights that "leave" before we needed to. Mom and Dad had a good laugh at that.

Finally, at 7:50 PM, a full ninety-five minutes after our original departure time, the plane began to taxi to its takeoff position.

The PA system came on. "Ladies and gentlemen, this is your captain speaking. My name is Natasha Reynolds, and with me tonight is First Officer Jeremy Bentsen. We apologize for the delays in getting this flight started, and we will strive to do our utmost to make it a pleasant one. We should be airborne within the next twenty minutes; if anyone has any questions, don't hesitate to ask. Thank you and enjoy the flight."

Eighteen minutes after leaving the gate, the plane was airborne and on our way to the Bluegrass state.

The first half of the flight was fairly uneventful. It was a beautiful night out, and the weather outside was calm, apart from a slight rattle that was barely noticed by the passengers.

But then, at 10:38 PM Central Time, as we were flying over Kansas City, something went wrong.

A loud bang rang out through the plane. There was a brief jolt, and the plane started vibrating up and down. I looked out the window to see what was happening.

I couldn't see anything unusual like wing damage or a malfunctioning engine or anything like that. But it seemed we were starting to fall to Earth.

The vibrations continued for seventeen minutes, and the plane was swerving from side to side like a pendulum.

Over the intercom, we heard Captain Reynolds scream "Brace for impact!"

The cabin crew chorused "Brace!" as everyone ducked down in their seats.

Finally, a loud thump resonated throughout the entity of the cabin, as if someone had shot a balloon with a nail gun. The plane had stopped shaking, and I noticed the plane was going down a runway.

Out the window on our side of the row, I could see a number of lights shoot to the left. The plane was still moving, but we were slowing down. Some people thought we were safe and started to sit back up, and I felt tempted to do the same.

"Stay down until we stop." Mom remained hunched in her brace position.

That's when we went off the end of the runway.

Three seconds later, at 10:55:28 PM, the plane hit the Missouri River, and skidded down the wooded riverbank.

The plane hit several trees, and the roof peeled open.

It took about thirty seconds to get my bearings. All four of us were still alive, and we were able to unbuckle ourselves and get out of our seats. As we regrouped, the surviving flight attendants opened the doors to evacuate the plane. The only light in the plane were from the flight attendants' flashlights, the full moon overhead, and the glow of arcing wires near the breaches in the fuselage.

The doors were all opened, and many started pouring out. Some people were trapped in their seats; others were too injured to get out of their seats, but still crying for help. And then there were some who were completely still. Many of the escaping passengers stopped to help the trapped and injured passengers to escape.

We all walked to the front of the plane to escape. As Mom jumped out, I caught a glimpse through the cockpit door which had fallen off the hinges. Through the doorway, I could see the pilots still strapped in their seats.

"Forte 934 heavy, this is Kansas City, do you read me?"

The sound of the air traffic controller on the radio lured me into the cockpit. Neither Captain Reynolds nor First Officer Bentsen were moving, but I could see their chests rising and falling. I could hear people calling out for help, but I noticed that the emergency services hadn't arrived yet.

I didn't know if they had been called at that point, so I got on the first officer's radio to try and call up the air traffic controller. "Kansas City, do you hear me?"

"Is this Forte 934 heavy?"

"Forte 934 heavy, affirmative."

"Forte 934 heavy, report the situation onboard."

"The plane has just crash landed in the river outside the airport. The flight crew appears to be unconscious, and we will need emergency services ASAP."

"Roger, Forte 934—wait, did you say the flight crew is unconscious?"

"Yeah, this is one of the passengers."

"Do you know what has happened with the plane?"

Outside, I heard a man shout. "Look! The vertical fin is on the runway!"

A female voice followed. "It looks like it split in half!"

I relayed the information. "It seems that the vertical stabilizer has split open. The plane had been shaking violently before it crashed, and the stabilizer appears to have fallen off upon the plane going off the runway."

"Do you know how many people are still alive?"

"Uh, negative, but it seems that there are a considerable number of survivors, and many of them are in need of urgent medical attention."

"Roger, standby and we'll get help."

At that moment, I heard a loud FWOOP. The flashes of white light from the arcing wires were overpowered by a bright yellow and orange light. I turned around and saw a fire burning through the second galley.

"I need to go now; a fire has broken out."

With that, I dropped the radio microphone and released the seat harnesses holding the pilots in their seats. I pushed the cockpit's windshield open and pushed the unconscious pilots out through the opening.

I climbed out behind them and dropped down to the mud below, where two of the flight attendants were standing, as well as seventy other passengers, six of whom were tending to the flight crew.

Further down the riverbank, I could see the vertical fin lying in the mud. The leading edge had indeed split in half, as if it had been partially cut in half lengthwise.

Around the nose of the smoldering plane, I could see forty-five more passengers, among them being Mom. A strip of metal was embedded in her left knee under the cap, and she was leaning on another passenger for support. I raced to her, and we embraced in a hug.

I had sustained several bruises in the impact, and I had cut myself while I was climbing out through the windshield. My clothes were torn and muddy, but aside from that, I was in decent shape.

Dad and Terrence were dragged out of the plane; both sustained serious burns. They had both gotten stuck trying to unbuckle themselves.

Three minutes after I made my way out of the plane, the emergency crews arrived. The firemen got to work on the fire, and everyone was escorted to Kansas City hospital for medical treatment.

Dad and I made a full recovery. Mom was left with a bad leg from her knee injury. Terrence died from his burns the morning after the accident.

Of the 187 passengers and 13 crew members that were on board, 70 passengers and 5 flight attendants perished; 28 were killed on impact, 36 died in the fire that followed, and 11 more died in the hospital. 117 passengers, 6 flight attendants, and both pilots survived.

Zelda monitored the investigation into the accident. On September 7th, 20—, she published a newspaper article which indicated a poor maintenance record by Firebird Airlines as the cause of the crash. As a result, the airline was charged with willful negligence, and the case went to court.

The verdict took the world by storm. Firebird Airlines was acquitted on all charges, while the mechanic who carried out the maintenance was shouldered with all responsibility and subsequently dismissed from his job.

Almost everyone around me was enraged at the court's lack of disciplinary action against Firebird Airlines.

Mom had gone through a decline in sanity in the years after the crash and subsequent trial.

Shannon became a recluse in her laboratory, appearing in public only with Richard or Zelda. She has displayed hints of animosity toward Alex and had concocted a drink mix that led Alex to become a bounty hunter at night.

For six months, even Alex's mood seemed to have been dampened somewhat. His spirits were lifted with the new trait catalyzed by Shannon; he was able to relieve his resentment without putting an end to his prank shop business.

I was the only one to not express hatred or a dramatic breakdown over the death of my brother or the acquittal of Firebird Airlines.

CHAPTER IV

The Journey

Satchel and I left the office and headed to the subway station. We stopped at Burger Barn for lunch before heading to the station. As we ate, Satchel and I discussed the past trials that ended badly.

"So, Mr. Satchel, who do you think is causing all of this mischief?"

"I'm not sure."

"If I had to guess, I'd say that someone is trying to keep their friends out of jail."

"The first flopped trials have dealt with civil cases. But I don't see how someone would try to circumvent a small fine. After all, it isn't really that much of a consequence."

"Hmm… good point."

"And whoever is behind this must have a widespread knowledge of how the justice system works."

"True. But that doesn't really give us a narrowed list of potential suspects; anyone could have a motive and knowledge of the court system."

"But who would have the capacity of carrying out such an audacious act?"

"I'm not sure. We may end up having to wait until they carry out another round of activity before we have any concrete evidence for all of this."

"And we still have to figure out why they are doing the things that they're doing."

"That's going to be challenging."

Satchel looked at his watch. "Oh! Look at the time! We should get going!"

"Yeah, we should do that." I wadded up my wrapper and threw it at a trash can. It bounced out, knocking napkins and cups out, and fell on the floor with a splat.

I went over to pick up all the garbage that fell out. The whole floor was a sticky mess of mustard and barbecue sauce, as well as some discarded cups and napkins. As I reached for the wrapper I threw, I noticed something odd.

Everything that was knocked out of the trash can was completely covered in sauce from the wrapper and lying in a messy pile. Yet on top of the wrapper, there was a neatly folded piece of white printer paper that had no sauce at all.

That couldn't have been there to start with; someone had to have slipped it there after it hit the floor. I looked around the pillar next to the can, but no one was there. Of course, there were dozens of people in the restaurant, so they could be in and out fairly quickly without notice.

I took the slip of paper out of the wrapper and unfolded it. There was a typed note on it:

So many court cases, so little time
And some never do pay the price for their crime
Today it shall start, a vengeful spree
Cold as ice, as you soon shall see
Horror and dread around
Every bend
Learning your life is nearing its end

8, 16, 4, 19, 14, 18, 23

I had no idea what that was supposed to mean, but I folded the note back up and put it in my pocket. Then I picked up all the garbage that had fallen out of the trash can and put it back where it was.

"Are you ready to head out, Johnson?"

"Yeah, I'm coming."

We walked out of the restaurant, and we headed for the subway station.

It was such a sudden jump going from a heated road to a chilly tunnel. We bought our tickets, made our way through the turnstile, and rode the escalator down to the platform.

The station was packed. I could barely see the edge of the platform past the jam-packed crowd of people. The noise of all the people talking was all I could hear in the tunnel. It was difficult to see Satchel through the crowd.

Fortunately, Satchel and I managed to stay together and make our way onto our train.

The train was even tighter than the platform. I could hardly move, and the train felt like an overinflated balloon.

During the ride, I thought about the note I had found.

I appeared to be in danger.

But how was I in danger?

And were my friends or family at risk as well?

Twenty minutes passed, and the train reached our stop. I got out of the train and headed up the escalator.

It was great to get into open space again. Though there was a lot more noise than in the subway.

That's when I realized something.

Satchel wasn't with me anymore.

I went back into the station and searched the platform up and down with no luck.

I boarded a train heading back to Landenberg and went searching through the stations that our train passed on the way to the police station.

I found myself back at the first station with no sign of Satchel anywhere.

I went up to the street to call Alex and organize my friends into a search party to look for him.

"Alex, I need your help. I was on my way to the police station with the defense attorney for the upcoming trial, but he is missing now."

"So, you lost a shoulder bag?"

"Ha ha, very funny. This isn't the time for jokes, Alex. Call up Richard, Shannon, and Zelda and have them meet me at the subway station."

"I'm on it."

All four of my friends were at the station in less than ten minutes.

I could recognize Alex very easily. His red-orange hair and checkered vest was unique to anything anyone wore or looked like. And his taped glasses and freckled face made his appearance all the more comic (at least during the day time when he was "Dr. Chuckle.").

If you didn't know that they were sisters, you would think Zelda and Shannon were close friends; Shannon was a blonde, and Zelda was a brunette. Richard and Patrick both had black hair (although Richard typically wears a baseball hat) so you could tell at first glance that they were brothers. Terrence and I were often mistaken as being twins, even though he was a few inches taller than me (despite the fact that I was older than him by about three years).

Shannon was the first to speak. "So, Johnson, what are we doing here?"

"I was meeting with William York's attorney, and he was called to the police station where he is being interrogated. But we got separated on the way there, and now he's gone. We need to go down to the subway and look for him."

When we arrived, we looked at the subway map to see which route Satchel and I had taken.

"Okay, so here's the police station," Richard pointed to a dot on the pink subway line, "and this is where we are right now." He pointed out the dot where an orange line crossed.

"The ride was twenty minutes long," I told them. "We both got on the train, but only I got off at our destination."

"So now the question," Zelda put a finger to her chin, "is where between the two stations did he get off?"

"There are signs visible from the windows," I pointed out, "and even if the platform was filled so full your blood couldn't circulate, you could still read them quite clearly."

Alex pondered that. "If he got off at the wrong stop, he must be really off track."

Shannon looked at the map. "So, there are four stops that we need to search."

There weren't as many people as before, but there was still a significant number. So, there was enough room that we were all able to see each other, unlike the trip with Satchel.

At the first stop, there was nothing. A man in a tuxedo did attract our attention for a brief moment, but we established that he wasn't who we were looking for.

We didn't find anything at the second stop either. The only thing that was out of the ordinary was that one of the escalators was undergoing maintenance work. Alex exchanged some talk with the mechanics before we continued.

At the third stop, I could see what looked like crime scene tape over the entrance to the area under the escalator, which was guarded by a uniformed officer. Each of us got off the train and headed over to investigate.

We were met by five more uniformed officers, one of whom I recognized immediately.

"Hey, Rachel, how's it going?"

Rachel Dinesen was a close cousin; we had gone to the same police academy, and we had used to play paintball with each other in high school. Her mother is my aunt and my boss, Police Chief Bethany Dinesen.

Rachel told the five other policemen to go to the crime scene, and then turned to me. "A dead body has been found back here. We haven't identified who it is yet."

"Is the body still there?"

"Yes, it is."

"Can I take a look? I might know who it is." I honestly did not want to say that.

"It's right up against the wall."

As I entered, I saw who was under the escalator and was shocked. Tied up in a bundle of extension cords was the body of Harold Satchel.

With a bloody puncture wound in his neck.

Chapter V

Murder #1

Each of us stood dumbfounded for about ten seconds, and then Richard spoke up. "How did this happen?"

"I wish I knew," Shannon responded.

Alex, Richard, Shannon, and Zelda went over to ask questions to the officers that were at the scene, while Rachel and I started talking.

"So, Johnson, what brings you here?"

"Well, Mr. Satchel and I were on our way to meet with William York during an interrogation. We got separated on the way there, and when my friends and I went to look for him, we stumbled across this crime scene."

"Well, as you found out, Satchel has been murdered."

"Yeah."

"So, can you tell me about what happened?"

"Well, I was helping Zelda with investigating a series of botched court cases, and I went to Satchel to hopefully get some clues."

"So, what made you decide to talk to William as well?"

"He would be serving as the defendant in the upcoming murder trial, and I've been told that he was involved in some other court cases. William happened to call his attorney during my interview with Satchel."

"Did anything unusual happen at all during your trip to the police station?"

"Well, we stopped for a bite to eat before heading to the subway. As we ate, we were discussing who would want to sabotage the court cases."

"Then what?"

"As Satchel and I were getting ready to leave, I dropped my wrapper on the floor. When I went to pick it up, I saw a perfectly clean, neatly folded piece of paper wedged into the saucy, crumpled up wrapper I had dropped. I picked it up out of the wrapper and unfolded it."

"What was on that piece of paper?"

"It looked like a poem. From what I think, it may have been a death threat from whoever was behind all the bad cases around here."

"Can I see it?"

I took the note out of my pocket and then handed it to Rachel. "Here you go."

"Thank you." She looked over the note with interest.

As she read, she looked as if she had read it before but couldn't remember where or when.

"Yeah, it does seem to be a death threat." She put the note in a bag. "I should have this looked at to see what, if anything, can be found."

"Alright. Good luck with that."

We shook hands, and we all went up to the street.

"You should probably talk to your father about this," Rachel suggested.

"Sure. I'll do that."

When I got to the apartment, I saw Mom and Dad were watching the news. On the TV, news reporters were on the scene broadcasting the story about Satchel's death.

"Hey, Mom. Hey, Dad."

"Hello, Johnson." Dad stood up and he escorted me to the living room.

Mom was waiting for me there. "Is there something you'd like to tell us about what happened this afternoon?"

"Martha, he's not in trouble."

"Sorry, Daniel; I'm just uneasy about this."

"Yes, I understand." Dad turned off the TV. "Anyway, how did your meeting go today?"

"Well, it ended on a very bad note."

"I figured that much."

"Satchel was killed in a subway tunnel as we were on our way to the police station. I told Rachel Dinesen about what had happened, and she explained what the crime scene looked like when she arrived."

"So, what happened to Satchel?"

"His body is being sent in for an autopsy. I was hoping the Thomson sisters and I could talk to the medical examiner that would be performing the autopsy."

"Alright. You do that."

I went to the phone to call Zelda.

"Hey, Johnson. What are you doing?"

"Hey, Zelda. I was going to see the medical examiner that would be performing Satchel's autopsy. I might need you and Shannon to come along with me."

"Sure thing, Johnson."

When we arrived, I saw Alex and Richard at the coffee shop across the street.

"Hey, Alex. What's up?"

"The porch canvas."

"Of course. So, what brings you here, Richard?"

"Alex and I were talking about the upcoming trial now that Satchel is dead."

"Yeah. We're going to interview the medical examiner that will be performing Satchel's autopsy to gather clues about his death."

"Okay. Well, good luck with that. If you need anything, Richard and I will be here."

"Good to know." With that, Zelda and I proceeded to enter the hospital.

I made my way to the receptionist's desk. She looked up from the computer at me. "Can I help you three?"

"Yes, we're here to talk to Dr. Arnold Suzuki." Zelda and I showed her our badges.

"Room 427 on the fourth floor."

"Alright, thank you, ma'am."

We headed to the stairwell and started up to the fourth floor, making our way to room 427.

I knocked on the door and waited for the door to be answered. A young man with black hair appeared.

Zelda presented her badge and then looked to the man. "Are you Dr. Arnold Suzuki?"

He nodded and spoke in a soft voice with a Japanese accent. "Yes, I am."

We gave out our hands for him to shake. "I'm Johnson Vasquez, and this is my partner Zelda Thomson, and her sister Shannon."

He shook hands with us and showed us into the room. "What may I do for you three?"

"My partner and I are investigating the death of Harold Satchel," Zelda started. "He was to be taking part in a murder trial in January. We understand that you were performing the autopsy on the victim."

"Yes. My findings are quite bizarre."

"How so?" I took note of the equipment that Dr. Suzuki was using for the autopsy on Satchel.

"Well, as you can see from my report," he showed me the report he had written up before we had showed up, "the cause of Mr. Harold Satchel's death I have determined to have been exsanguination from a breach in the jugular vein. And it appears he has been stabbed with a large sharp object, perhaps a stake or something of a similar nature."

"So, what did you find bizarre?" Shannon asked.

"What I found so bizarre, Ms. Thomson, was that the weapon seems to have broken when it was inserted into the damaged area. You would think, therefore, that a piece of the weapon would have been lodged somewhere in the area. But that simply is not the case. And there is no indication that the broken off piece was ever removed, or that anyone ever tried to take it out."

"So, the broken piece simply vanished?" I wrote down what Dr. Suzuki had been saying.

"So, what happened?" Zelda took off her hat briefly to cool herself down.

"Allow me to explain." He walked to the closet and brought out a half-"dissected" mannequin to demonstrate what he was telling us. "The killing was reminiscent of sharpening a pencil; the weapon was inserted just below the lower jaw, splitting the vein. From there, death was inevitable. The force was equal to pushing a pencil through an index card, but it was enough to break the tip of the weapon that was used."

"Were you able to figure out what kind of weapon was used?" Zelda hoped to find some sort of lead as to who had killed the legendary attorney.

"As I said before, it was something like a stake. But it was so brittle that it broke with very little force, and there were no traces to be found in the area. So, I do not know what kind of material the weapon was made of."

"What kind of stake breaks with hardly any force? And if it broke, why are there no fragments to be found?" I wrote the information in my pad, intending to figure out what kind of weapon killed Satchel.

Dr. Suzuki then pointed out another puzzle. "There's something else strange: despite the fact that Mr. Satchel bled to death, none of his clothes had any blood at all. The only blood on the body was a crescent shaped puddle just one inch below the puncture wound."

Shannon looked at it closely. "If you think about it, it's almost like part of a perfect circle."

"Hm. It sort of looks that way."

"Perhaps if we had a copy of the report, we can study it more closely for evidence."

Dr. Suzuki understood the request, and supplied us with a copy of the report, as well as pictures taken of the body.

"Thank you for your time, Dr. Suzuki."

"You're welcome, Mr. Vasquez."

Zelda turned to me as we left the office. "We should probably talk to the others about this."

"I agree."

CHAPTER VI

Discussion

When Zelda, Shannon, and I emerged from the hospital, Richard and Alex were still outside at the coffee shop.

Richard pulled up seats for the three of us. "So, what'd you find at the autopsy?"

"I wish I knew." Zelda took her seat next to Shannon.

"What do you mean?" Alex took a sip from his caramel latte and said, "Was what you found confusing you?"

"No, it was what we didn't find." I scanned the menu on the table.

"What do you mean 'what you didn't find?'" Richard put down his hot chocolate.

"Dr. Suzuki says he was stabbed in the neck, and the stake appears to have broken and disappeared." I started to slide down in my seat.

Alex tried to cheer me up. "Well, just because the stake went to pieces doesn't mean you have to go to pieces."

Rachel came up to the café, and Zelda and I went over to talk to her.

"Hey, Rachel." We shook hands with each other.

Rachel, Zelda, and I went over to sit on the bench on the sidewalk to have a discussion.

"So, about that note I gave you…"

"Yes. I'm afraid that I wasn't able to discern very much evidence from it." She pulled it from her pocket.

"No?" I took the note back from her.

"The only fingerprints I was able to find on that note were yours, but you had read that note, so that doesn't tell me anything."

Zelda looked at the poem. "What about what the poem itself said?"

"I hadn't had a chance to read it more closely."

"I'm going to take a look at it." Zelda took the note and started reading it.

Rachel and I went inside the café while Zelda returned to the table to examine the note.

"So, Johnson, how's life treating you?"

"Aside from the murder that took place today, I've been pretty great."

"Yeah. Are your friends all good?"

"Yes, they are."

"I haven't talked to Rickey in a long time."

"Yeah, Richard has been busy lately."

"Is he still doing baseball?"

"Yep. He still is. He's expressed interest in joining the Major Leagues someday."

"That sounds fun. How's he doing with Shannon?"

"They seem like a perfect match."

"Yeah?"

"Richard and Shannon have become better people since they started being together."

"I see. What about Alex?"

"He's been doing great."

"Has he noticed anything unusual happening around his store at all?"

"He hasn't said anything about that. Why?"

"My colleagues were telling about rumors at that place; I thought I'd ask you about that."

"Okay. Well, I have nothing to report about that. Nothing unusual that I've noticed other than plans for a bowling alley."

"And Zelda's been steady with you?"

"Oh yeah."

"That's good."

"Well, I should probably regroup with my friends. It's been great talking with you, Rachel."

"You too, Johnson."

As I sat back down at the table, Zelda looked over at me. "There are lots of clues in this note. I don't know how it's possible that Rachel could've overlooked them."

"Yeah, there are plenty of clues to be had." We started pointing out those clues.

"This is what the first two lines say: 'So many court cases, so little time / And some never do pay the price for their crime.' So, whoever wrote this must be the mastermind behind this injustice string."

"'Today it shall start, a vengeful spree / Cold as ice as you soon shall see.' That doesn't make sense; if they're behind the sour justice debacle, how could their 'vengeful spree' be starting today?"

"Well, it could indicate a new line of revenge. Perhaps it has escalated toward killing people."

"And what is 'cold as ice' supposed to mean? Are they trying to say 'cold-blooded' or...?"

"It could very well be that."

"And the last line is 'Horror and dread around / Every bend / Learning your life is nearing its end.'"

"That would confirm a death threat from whoever wrote this." Zelda was emphatic about this remark.

"It seems strange that 'Horror and dread around / Every bend' is written on two lines."

"Well, if you look at the spine, it reads SATCHEL."

"Interesting. So, what could these numbers mean?"

Zelda shrugged.

Shannon rubbed her eyes and picked up the note. "Does anyone know who wrote this?"

"I don't know," Alex answered, "but they sure do write some killer poetry."

Shannon was the only one who didn't laugh. Richard pounded the table so hard that Zelda's milkshake fell off the table. The shattering of the glass quieted all of us.

A waitress came over with a mop, sweep, and dustpan within ten seconds. As she cleaned up the glass shards, Alex tried to lighten the mood.

"Kind of makes you wish they made cups out of ice. It would keep the drink cool, and if you dropped it, the pieces would melt away without a trace."

That's when a Eureka moment struck. I quickly looked back at the autopsy report, then to the ice on the floor, and then I looked at Alex. With a jubilant beam, I felt the urge to hug him right then and there.

Thankfully, I didn't.

"What are you so happy about, Johnson?"

"I think I have an idea of what might have happened. I'll test my theory tonight at my parents' house, and if it seems to be what we're looking for, I'll gather everyone over there tomorrow morning."

"Can you tell us what you think it was?"

"Not at this point; I need to make sure it was actually possible before I reveal it. I'll talk to my dad about it."

Richard shrugged. "Alright."

It was late when I got to Mom and Dad's apartment. They were in the midst of a candlelit dinner.

"Oh, sorry. Am I interrupting?"

Mom shook her head. "Not at all. We were just about to start cleaning up."

Dad gathered the plates and glasses. "So, what brings you here tonight, son?"

"I wanted to talk to you about my findings in regard to Satchel's murder." I glanced over at Mom. "Would it be alright if Dad and I talked in private?"

"Certainly, you may do that. I'll be over in the kitchen cleaning up."

"Alright." Dad and I went to the back porch.

Once the two of us were outside, I briefed Dad on the newest information. "I think I have an idea of how Satchel was killed today."

"How's that?"

"I think he had been stabbed with an icicle."

"How do you figure that?"

I showed him the autopsy report. "The M.E. told us that Satchel had been stabbed in the neck with some kind of stake. The tip broke off when it was used, but there was no sign of the missing piece in the wound, nor was there evidence of anyone trying to remove it."

"I see." He looked at some of the other details. "It also says that there was almost no blood at all outside of the body, even though Satchel bled to death."

"Yeah. We weren't able to figure out why that was."

He pointed out the crescent shape that Shannon noticed. "The puddle seems almost like part of a perfect circle, kind of like a coffee mug stain on a table."

"What I want to know is whether or not it's possible to kill someone by stabbing them with an icicle."

"Well, since Satchel was stabbed in the jugular vein, it would be easy for a rupture to cause almost total blood loss and death. The killer would've had to find a way to first of all make an icicle that was sharp enough to cause the necessary damage, and also find out how it would stay frozen long enough to be used to kill someone."

"And it's obvious that the icicle has melted, leaving no evidence at all as to the icicle's dimensions."

"I would think that the icicle would've had to have been formed during the winter; there's not that much of an effective alternative method to do that. It would've had to be perhaps twelve to fifteen inches long to have the necessary shape. There would also have to be a means by which the icicle stayed frozen until it was ready to use."

"You mean like a cooler with dry ice? Because I don't think that would store well in a standard freezer, given how much other stuff would be in there with it. Plus, a power cut would risk allowing the ice to melt."

It was then that Mom opened the porch door. "Bethany called me; she says she wants the two of you to be into work at 6 AM tomorrow. So, you should probably get home and get some rest, Johnson."

"Would it be at all possible for me to spend the night here so that Dad and I can continue our discussion?"

"That's fine with me. The spare bedroom is available."

"Okay." I went to the closet where Mom and Dad kept the sleeping bags and picked one to use for the night.

"Alright." Mom headed to her bedroom to get ready for bed. "Goodnight, Johnson."

"Goodnight."

Chapter VII

Alex's Story

Hey, this is Alex Andrews. Sorry for this interruption, I just thought I'd add my own narrative to this story. Richard, Shannon, and Zelda will be adding their own narratives as well later in this novel. Johnson will pick back up after this chapter, but for now, I'll be talking here; so just bear with me before you go grizzly.

As Johnson has probably told you, I'm a close friend of his. He has probably mentioned the fact that I have two states of mind; one during the day and one during the night. Now you might be wondering how I can live two separate lives that are almost exact opposites. Well, that I shall tell you right now.

You've probably visited my gag shop on Fischer Blvd, Dr. Chuckle's Prank Lab and Gag Shop. There's the orthodox collection of what you would expect to find in a store like this; there are whoopee cushions, rubber chickens, squirting flowers, hand buzzers, etc. I also have costume props, stuffed animals, magic sets, party decorations, and crazy drink ingredients.

None of my regular customers have any idea that I have a "secret" identity. They only know me as a redheaded geek with an extremely nerdy appearance and sharp sense of humor. What they don't realize is that when the sun sets, my entire persona metamorphoses.

The only people that know the connection between me and my nighttime alter-ego are Johnson, Richard, Shannon, and Zelda. You would never recognize me if you saw me running around after dusk.

My red-orange hair is hidden with a black toboggan hat. In place of my taped glasses is a pair of night-vision goggles. My yellow and green checkered shirt is concealed under a black turtleneck and bullet-proof vest. Where my suspenders would be is a sleeveless army jacket with three pockets on either side. Instead of wearing red and yellow sneakers, I have black army boots.

What you see before you is the bounty hunter Brandon Fuhrman Chide.

Now why would I, being a playful and silly prank shop owner, take on an almost bipolar change during the hours of the evening? You may very well ask that.

As Johnson explained, his younger brother, Terrence, was one of 75 people killed on Firebird Airlines Flight 934. He also said that Firebird Airlines was acquitted of failing to supervise a maintenance operation in which the head mechanic used a damaged rivet to complete a maintenance operation on Flight 934's vertical fin. I, like thousands of people, knew the airline itself was at fault, not the head mechanic, who lost his job because of the crash. But the attorney representing Firebird Airlines was widely celebrated, and the exclusionary rule left key evidence ignored, which led to a partisan case in favor of the airline.

I knew there was injustice in play at the courtroom, but the decision had been made, and nothing could change it. I felt incensed; to suffer a catastrophic loss, and then the guilty ones get away clean. I knew this couldn't be left at this. I wanted to do something about this, but I was not willing to give up my success at my store.

Late one Friday evening, I was in the basement of my store working on a comedy routine. My friends, who had not yet graduated, (this was six months after Firebird Airlines was acquitted) were with me to offer their help.

Shannon, who had a strong dislike for me, was at that time taking chemistry classes under the education of Professor Martha Ida Laverne Vasquez, Johnson's mother. She was at the drink station running a series of tests on some chemicals she had received earlier that day in the mail.

Shannon was attempting to find a cure for her weak-willed demeanor; she has been tormented with pusillanimity ever since the incident which ultimately inspired Johnson to go into the police department. And after the trial about Firebird Airlines Flight 934, she has spent almost all her time locked up in her lab, only going out in public with Richard and Zelda.

After what had to be sixty-three tests and experiments, Shannon finished up her work.

Richard decided to mix up a batch of my signature punch at Shannon's request. Richard is my best friend, and he is the only other person that knows the recipe for the punch.

Shannon wanted Firebird Airlines to pay for what they did. She said whoever finds a way to avenge Flight 934 should be toasted. We agreed, and then after we said cheers, we all at once downed each cup in one breath.

For twenty seconds, nothing seemed out of place. Then suddenly, we all fell to the floor clutching our stomachs and moaning in pain. Before I could pick myself up, I was quickly struck down by a splitting headache. I passed out on the floor, and as I did so, I could see the broken glasses where everyone dropped them.

When I regained consciousness, five minutes had gone by. I was still in the store's basement, as were my friends, who all appeared to have woken up as well. Everything was exactly as it was when the incident happened, but there was something seriously amiss.

The first thing I noticed was that everyone had changed appearances. We were all in darker mindsets.

Johnson was a drill sergeant. He was dressed in forest camouflage and his face was covered in dirt and scars.

I had become a bounty hunter. I looked in the reflection of the glass staircase door, and I saw what appeared to be a CIA agent standing where I was.

Richard was a rock guitarist. He had bright purple hair, and everything else he wore was either black or neon green.

The biggest change was Shannon; she appeared to be a cross between a monkey and a lion.

And Zelda had become an army commander (albeit not overbearing).

Both females had even taken a masculine shift.

We were quick to discern our situation, and pretty soon we realized the punch was spiked. Richard soon found out that he had added a wrong ingredient; an empty vial was found in the cabinet near the lab station. In the vial were coarse crystals similar to sugar. That was never there from what I remember.

Shannon came forward. She confessed to having made the flavoring we had all been doped with.

I heard some commotion upstairs and went to check it out. Everyone else I instructed to stay put.

When I reached the top, I heard someone was walking around through the shop. I quietly hid behind the counter as the burglar roamed around.

A flashlight beam shone across the room, searching for something to take. When it reached the counter where I was hiding, it stopped. I then heard footsteps approaching; they had no idea that I was behind the cash register.

I reached for a gun under my jacket and watched as a hand wedged a chisel into the register drawer.

That's when I sprung into his face, gun pointed straight at his widened eyes.

He instinctively took a few steps backwards, and then sprinted straight out the door screaming at the top of his lungs.

I vaulted over the counter, smashed through the front window to trigger the alarm, and followed him down the lamp-lit street.

He tried to rush down side alleys to get me off his trail, but he couldn't shake me. Several times he tried to overturn trash barrels to barricade my progress, but the efforts were in vain. At one point, he threw his chisel at me, but no damage was taken.

Finally, I trapped him outside of an apartment complex. There was no place left to run.

Keeping my gun pointed at him, I fished out a pair of handcuffs. "Turn around and face the wall, and put your hands behind your back."

He obeyed, and I proceeded to handcuff him.

I led him back to the shop, where the police had arrived to investigate.

"Good morning, officers." I presented them with the robber. "I just caught this man trying to rob this store."

The thief was taken to the squad car by one of the cops, and the other one turned his attention to me. "Now who are you and what were you doing here at night outside of the shop's business hours?"

I was quick to concoct a cover story. "Name's Chide. Brandon Chide. The store's owner had asked me to guard the shop during closing hours; this is my first night on the job."

"So, who is the owner of the store?"

"His name is Alex Darren Lucius Andrews. If you want him to verify my story, you're going to have to wait for him to call you; you're not going to find him at this hour."

"How would he know to call for an interview?"

"I'll be sure to tell him everything. He trusts me with everything in his possession."

I could read the suspicious skepticism on his face. "Uh-huh. I'm just going to wait here until Mr. Andrews shows up."

"Suit yourself." I went back downstairs and regrouped with the others.

By the time morning came around, the mixture's effects had worn off. If you had walked in on us at that point in time, you would never have known that anything unusual had ever taken place.

We went upstairs and saw the squad car parked outside the store. My friends went their separate ways while I woke up the policeman asleep at the wheel.

After I confirmed the story that I had told him the night before, he left without incident, oblivious that he had talked to the same person twice.

Following that night, I found I was alternating between two people throughout the day; Dr. Franklin Benson Chuckle by day, and Mr. Brandon Fuhrman Chide by night.

And thus, it began: the strange case of Dr. Chuckle and Mr. Chide.

Chapter VIII

Wainwright Law

The next morning, something was amiss at breakfast.

"Hey, Mom, where's Dad?"

"I don't know."

"I had tried calling him this morning, but there was no answer; it went straight to voicemail."

"Hm. Well, I'm sure you'll see him later today."

"I sure hope so."

Mom brought out pancakes, and as she sat down, she spilled her coffee on her shirt. "Augh!"

"You okay, Mom?"

"Yeah, I'm fine. Could you go to my closet and get me another shirt?"

"I'm on it." I left and went to Mom and Dad's closet.

When I got there, I saw something on the floor. A large tangle of wires and extension cords was lying in the corner that was furthest from the door.

There was also a cardboard box filled with small clear plastic bags. All of them were empty, but it had me wondering why they were in my parents' closet.

I picked out a shirt and went to the laundry room where Mom was.

I handed Mom the shirt. "Here you go."

"Thank you." She shut the door and proceeded to take off the old shirt.

Within a minute, she walked back out just as she was pulling the new shirt down across her stomach, which had a big bruise on it that almost looked like a footprint.

I wasn't sure whether or not to say anything about it, so I decided to say nothing.

"Did you sleep well last night, Johnson?"

"Uh, yeah, I did."

"That's good."

The rest of breakfast went by without incident.

Afterward, I rounded up everyone to head back to the subway station. Before we left, we had a talk on the sidewalk in front of the apartment complex.

"So, what are we doing?" Shannon didn't know why I suddenly went from frustrated to enthusiastic in a few seconds at the café.

"I think I know what the murder weapon is."

"What was it?" Richard asked me.

"I think Satchel had been stabbed with an icicle."

"It's the first week of October, and it's been sunny for at least twelve days; it's too warm for icicles to form." Zelda was skeptical about my conclusion.

"Perhaps they got it last winter and were saving it?" I thought it seemed a reasonable explanation.

Alex thought the idea was ludicrous. "So, one minute the investigation is on ice, the next we're *really* dealing with a cold-blooded killer?"

I heard Mom laughing. "It looks like it."

I turned around. "You heading out?"

"Yep." She kissed my forehead. "Hopefully, your father will turn up soon."

As she left, Zelda gave me a confused look.

"Dad wasn't home this morning, and I couldn't call him on his cell phone."

"Hm…"

That's when I felt a piece of paper under my shirt.

I took it out and looked at it. How did that suddenly appear seemingly out of nowhere?

"Does anyone know where this came from?"

The simultaneous answer from all four that were with me was unanimous. "No."

I unfolded the piece of paper and was instantly struck by a shocking déjà vu. There was another typed poem on it.

Very unnerving (pardon the pun)
And yet I'm afraid it has only begun
So be you nimble and
Quick, double quick
Up and jump over the candlestick
Ere you face this man with a broken shin
Zachary Jacques Tolono Venshlin

3, 25, 2, 6, 17, 27, 13

I immediately showed it to Zelda. There was a sense of foreboding settling on the lawn.

The other three read the poem as well.

Richard was confused. "How is 'unnerving' supposed to be a pun?"

Alex, being the humor expert, was able to understand it. "You know that 'unnerving' means shockingly scary. It's also a reference to Satchel, who is dead and therefore no longer has nerve activity."

Shannon looked at the middle lines. "There's obviously a 'Jack Be Nimble' reference right there."

Zelda looked at the name that was scribed at the bottom of the note. "Who's Zachary Venshlin?"

I recognized that name. "Satchel had mentioned him at our meeting; he said that he was recently hired at the firm, and that Satchel would be showing him the ropes. But that's all I know about him."

Richard also seemed to have knowledge about him. "I think Patrick had said something about him; he said he would be taking part in the upcoming trial. He might be replacing Satchel as the defense attorney."

It was then that I read the spine as VASQUEZ. "You don't suppose Venshlin is behind all this, do you?"

Nobody knew what to say.

The silence was broken by loud yet faint sounds which I recognized as fire sirens.

Suddenly, we saw three fire trucks speed past us. As we looked in the direction they were going, we saw a large smoke plume rising from the center of town.

Zelda hopped in the squad car, closely followed by me and the other three. We sped off after the fire engines to see what was going on.

Within minutes, we found the source of the smoke: the Wainwright Law Academy downtown was on fire. There were nearly a thousand students and teachers gathered outside the smoldering building. They all watched the black smoke lick out of the windows in awestruck terror.

I walked up to a man who I assumed was the school's administrator and asked him, "What's going on here?"

"A fire has broken out in the school!" The look on his face told me he thought this was arson.

"Do you know where the fire started?" I took out my notepad to write down the notes.

"There was a student on the second floor of the south wing that reported fire coming from a closet."

I turned to look at the people surrounding the south wing to see who it could have been, and then I looked back to the administrator. "Do you know where they are right now?"

He looked around and pointed to a fountain with thirty people gathered around it. "He's the one with the blue jacket and the red tie."

Most of the fire was put out, but the job was far from over. I walked over to the man I was pointed out.

He looked to me and spoke without hesitation. "Oh, thank goodness you're here! Someone has just tried to destroy the school building!"

Zelda tried to calm him down. "Sir, we'll help you as best we can; just tell us what you saw."

I took out my notepad. "The administrator said that you were the first person to notice the fire, is that correct?"

"Yeah. I was leaving my classroom in the south wing to go to the restroom. The restrooms on the third floor were out of service, so I went to the second floor. As I reached the bottom of the stairs, I smelled something burning; and as I approached the restrooms, the smell became worse. I also started to hear a crackling sound, and there were puffs of smoke billowing from under the closet door between the restrooms.

"I tried to open the door, but the handle was too hot. I quickly established that a fire was burning on the other side of the door. I hurriedly ran to the nearest fire alarm and pulled it as quickly as I could.

"By the time everyone had made it out of the building, the south wing's entire second floor was ablaze. I was able to find the administrator and I explained to him where the fire had started. The fire services arrived ten minutes later, followed by you two." He pointed to me and Zelda.

I wrote down everything he told me. "I see. Was there any suspicious activity prior to the fire?"

He shook his head. "Not to my knowledge."

"Do you know if anyone else saw anything suspicious in the minutes before the fire?"

"No, I don't."

Zelda rubbed her chin. "We should probably take a look inside once the fire is out."

I closed my notepad and looked up at what was left of the building. "There doesn't seem to be too much structural damage to the building; it shouldn't be too risky to investigate the scene."

It was twenty minutes before the firemen were satisfied that all the fire was gone and that the building was safe for us to investigate. By then, everyone was accounted for, and many people had already gone home.

Zelda and I went up to the fire chief. "Is it safe to go in there and search for clues?"

He nodded. "Go ahead. But be very careful."

Armed with flashlights and gloves, Zelda and I entered the building through the south wing's rear door. The scene inside was stark.

There was no light bar the sunlight coming through the windows. There were no burns on the first floor, but a thin mist of stagnant smoke filled the enclosed space. The ceramic floor was covered in fine ceiling debris, and clocks on the walls were at twenty minutes past seven.

The second floor was even more fearsome. The walls had sustained damage, and the concrete under the plaster was visible. The covers on the clocks were cracked, and the hands were stopped at five minutes past seven. And everything, I mean everything, was covered in a thick coat of soot. So thick, you'd think it was black to begin with.

A pile of ashes near the restrooms confirmed the story we had been told.

At first, it didn't seem to be arson, since there weren't any foul smells such as gasoline, kerosene, or anything that an arsonist would use to start a fire. When we went inside of the closet, we made a frightening discovery.

A human figure tied to a water pipe. On his chest was a police badge, which was undamaged by the fire but covered in soot. I brushed the soot off the badge with my thumb—and nearly dropped dead.

The badge identified the body as my father, Daniel Jack Vasquez.

CHAPTER IX

Murder #2

Zelda immediately radioed the station. "This is Zelda Thomson. A dead body has been found at Wainwright Law Academy. We need backup."

I sighed and casually turned to my right, where I saw a steel box. I opened it, and I saw a book cover. It was opened toward us, and it was clear that someone had ripped out all the pages. The inside of the back cover had a note written on it in red marker.

First it was cold, this time it was hot
Is this the end? I'm afraid not
Really the answer is in your possession
Easy to find with your new obsession
But there is still business left that's unfinished
I must now wait 'til the chase has diminished
Read this and ask yourself "Can it be so?"
Doubtful about what you want to know

I turned it over to look at the front. On the cover it said "Boeing 767-200 Training Manual."

Zelda found a soft lump of purple stuff on top of the charred corpse, still hot from the fire.

I turned to look at it. "What is it?"

Zelda rubbed her finger on it. "It looks like it's wax."

That was a thought provoking find.

Zelda read the poem on the flight manual cover, and then looked at the outside.

While she did this, I took pictures of the inside of the closet. There was hardly any hope that they would be useful, but we had to do what we had to do. I also took samples for Shannon to test to see if this was arson.

Zelda started wondering about the flight manual cover I had found. "This could be a crucial piece of evidence."

I examined what was left of my dad's clothes. There were only flakes on the scorched flesh, but some of the flakes were crispier than the others. Those flakes weren't from flesh or clothing; they were pieces of paper.

I showed the flakes to Zelda. "I think I found out what happened to all the pages of the training manual."

Zelda seemed bemused. "Where exactly did they get an airplane training manual?"

"I don't know." I looked at the watch on Dad's wrist, which showed a time of 6:52 AM.

"So, the fire took hold 13 minutes after it was set?"

"Seems like it."

"So, how did the fire burn outside the closet?"

"We're here to investigate this murder, not the fire."

"Well, we did find the place where the fire started."

I suddenly remembered something. I took out the poem I had received outside the store and reread it. "I should have known. This explains everything. It explains the circumstances of my dad's death, it explicitly says my dad's name, and it says who killed him."

Zelda spotted my broiling anger. "Maybe you're acting a bit hastily, Johnson."

I took no note of her words as I crumpled the note in my fist. "I will find him if it's the last thing I do."

I was about to run out of what was left of the building when three of my colleagues appeared at the door, among them being Rachel.

"I should have known it was you."

I was flabbergasted. "What?"

"You thought you could hide your tracks so easily, did you? Well, I got news for you, chump: that ain't happening."

"What kind of cop do you think you are?"

Rachel took out her notepad and flipped through the pages. "I spoke with your friends down in the courtyard, and Rickey told me about your theory about how you think Satchel was murdered. You say that he was stabbed with an icicle, did you not?"

I exhaled through my nose. "The medical examiner had explained that a piece of the weapon broke off in Satchel's neck, and it had vanished by the time the body was examined. From that, as well as a joke from Alex, I was able to deduce that the weapon was made of ice."

Rachel shot a suspicious stare at me. "I've known you for all my life. There's no way you could have come to that conclusion that quickly unless you committed the crime."

"I didn't!"

"And what about that note you 'found' in the restaurant you and Satchel went to? I thought your fingerprints on that note didn't mean anything. Well, now I know that it was you who wrote this."

"How could I have come up with something like that?" I was about to slap her across the face, but Zelda grabbed my wrist before I did anything.

"And how is it you ended up here at the place that your father died at while the fire was burning?"

"I had happened to hear sirens, and we drove over to see what was going on."

"And isn't it interesting how your father was a great detective?"

"Yeah, I'm sure that he was murdered to protract the investigation into Satchel's murder. But that doesn't mean I killed him."

"There's no question that Danny's profession makes him a target for anyone looking to cover their tracks. But not many people have the means or the knowledge to go after Danny, especially in this manner. And the time of disappearance from his apartment was last night."

"And you think I'm the only one that could've done it?"

There was a long pause, and then Rachel changed the subject. "Mind if I ask why you didn't stay in the high school drama club?"

It seemed an absurd question (and likely intended to be some sort of an accusation) but I decided to answer it anyway. "I only got cast in two plays during the entire time that I was involved."

"You had a part in *Ten Little Warriors*, right?"

"Yeah; I had the role of Anthony Marston."

"And if I recall correctly, you had also acted in *Othello*, is that right?"

"Yes, I did. Terrence and I both had roles in that play. I played Cassio, and Terrence played Iago."

"I'd say you two were perfect for the roles. Your acting was impressive; it was as if you were just being your real-life selves onstage. Anyway, I digress."

"So, what's your point?"

"You seem to have a talent for acting, since you are pretending to have nothing to do with these crimes which you committed."

"I didn't! I can tell you right now who did it."

"Fine, then. Who is it?"

I took a step toward her. "Zachary Venshlin."

Rachel rested her hand on her chin. "Never heard of the guy. Care to elaborate?"

"All I know is that he's a criminal defense attorney who is working at the Landenberg Law Firm."

"And why do you suspect him of these crimes?"

I reached into my pocket and took out the note I found before going to Wainwright. "Does this ring any bells?"

Rachel looked at it, and then looked up to me. "Hmm… it would seem like it. I'm going to go talk to the Wainwright faculty to see what they know about this Venshlin character and possible motives."

I put the note in my pocket. "I'll have my friends and me look at this mystery, and we'll get to the bottom of this."

"Alright, if that's how you'll play, I'm fine with that. But I'll be one step ahead of you, Vasquez Private Eye."

After we left the burned building, we met back up with Alex, Richard, and Shannon at our cruiser.

"So, did you find out where the fire started?" Shannon looked up from her watch.

Zelda started up the cruiser, and we began to drive off. "Johnson's father was cremated near one of the restrooms."

Richard was taken aback. "Are you serious?"

I responded immediately. "Yeah. He was tied to a water pipe, stuffed with the pages of an airplane training manual, and then burned alive."

My anger really began to broil from a combination of Dad's murder and Rachel's browbeating. "And I can tell you right now that the culpability lies with—"

"Whoa, calm down, Johnson." Alex patted me on the shoulder. "There's no need to burn yourself up."

I took a few deep breaths. "So, let's see if we can piece together what took place at Wainwright."

Shannon sifted through the samples we had collected. "Well, until we get the autopsy results for your father, we have no way to know if he was killed in the fire or before it."

Richard started pondering. "So, what did you find?"

"Well, the fire started in the closet where Dad had been found dead. Zelda found what seemed to be wax on top of the body, and his clothes were stuffed with paper. There was also a steel box with an airplane training manual cover which had had all of the pages torn out."

Shannon read the poem written on the inside cover we had collected, and the way she reacted you'd think that she was walking through a slaughterhouse.

As she read, Richard spoke up. "So, why did the killer choose Wainwright to kill your father at?"

"I don't know. We'll have to do some studying. Zelda, Shannon, and I will talk to the medical examiner to figure out what happened to my dad. Richard, you try to find out as much about Wainwright as you can to see what connection, if any, Venshlin has to it. And Alex, you review all of the evidence from Satchel's murder we have so far."

Everyone acknowledged their roles.

"Excellent. Let's get to work, and we'll meet at Alex's store this evening."

CHAPTER X

Cops Compete

I thought about what Rachel said to me at Wainwright.

"I'll be one step ahead of you, Vasquez Private Eye."

I had no idea what that was supposed to mean. From the way Rachel said it, it seemed that she was mocking me for not being an official investigator in the murders.

But I might also have an advantage point for what kind of evidence I could collect. I wasn't an official investigator, so I had little need for a warrant to search for evidence.

Somehow, I felt that there was a third meaning to it, but I didn't quite know what it was.

Dr. Suzuki had his hands full; he had the epic task of examining the body for any pre-fire injuries. And Shannon was running tests on blood samples, as well as trying to determine the origin of the fire.

"So, what have you found so far, Dr. Suzuki?" I asked.

"Well, there's no evidence to suggest that he had been injured before the fire; the only thing I can find to have existed prior to the fire are a series of chafe marks around the wrists and ankles."

"So, that would mean he was struggling between the time he was bound and when the fire was started." Zelda was amazed at how much of the body was recovered.

Shannon was examining the materials recovered from the crime scene. "He may have been wearing only boxers and a white T-shirt, so that would suggest he was abducted the night previous to the fire."

"Yes. Once we get the blood test results, we can figure out whether he was dead or alive at the time of the fire."

While we waited, I studied the X-rays taken earlier by Dr. Suzuki. The body was intact, so if there was evidence of a struggle, we could find it.

None of the ribs showed signs of scratches or fractures, indicating that he wasn't stabbed or beaten before the fire.

The X-rays showed no signs of any physical trauma at all that could've happened before death.

I studied the whittled flesh that had escaped the blaze. "So, judging by the fact that there's no fire damage where the binds were, it would seem that they were made of a material that doesn't burn easily."

Zelda looked to Shannon. "Do you know if he had been drugged or poisoned before being taken to Wainwright?"

"We'll have to wait for the blood test results; then we can know who the victim was, and if he died in the fire, or if he was killed beforehand."

I gave the X-rays back to Dr. Suzuki. "The chafes on the wrists and ankles seem a bit deep to have been caused by waking up in the closet and struggling to get loose."

"True. And we'd need to see what had been used to tie him up."

Shannon examined the charred ropes and noticed that they were extension cords. The outer insulation had flaked off, exposing the metallic weave that shielded the individual color-wrapped wires in the core.

Shannon noticed the nature of the damage. "I think the cord scraped something. It might have been a zipper."

Zelda was quick to intervene. "Let's wait until we have all the evidence before we try to draw conclusions."

"Good idea."

It was about that time that the results came back. The DNA test confirmed that the charred body was indeed that of my father.

There were no abnormal chemicals in the blood content except for a high concentration of carbon monoxide.

And I'm talking *high* concentration.

"So, he *was* killed during the fire."

Shannon nodded. "And it wouldn't seem he had been drugged or poisoned beforehand."

"So, whoever killed him must have known how to and been able to overpower him enough to tie him up."

"But what caused the fire to start in the first place?"

"The others are probably waiting for us at Alex's store; the rest of the tests will have to wait until later. Let's head over there and see what we can find out."

"Alright." Zelda turned to address Dr. Suzuki. "Thank you for your time."

"You're welcome."

At Alex's store, each of us five shared the information we had accrued.

"So, Richard, what did you find out about Wainwright Law Academy?"

"The law academy was built in 1965, and it was opened to the public in August of that year."

"Do you have any information about who had studied at Wainwright or if there was anything to forestall the fire there?"

"There were a few students with reports of a mysterious figure going in and out of an alley on the academy's south side, but no one knows who it could be, or even if the stories are true or false."

"Hm. What about the students and alumni there?"

"The school was highly prestigious, so it was extremely rare for students to leave a legacy at Wainwright. But there was one who stood out as a dedicated student." Richard looked to a note he had. "Ah. Here it is. Zachary Venshlin."

It was a shock to learn that someone who I suspected of rigging court cases and killing two people had been a superstar student at Wainwright.

I turned to Shannon. "Hey, Shannon, have you finished up those tests yet?"

She had seemed squeamish about Richard talking about the story of the alley behind Wainwright. But she led us to the drink station where she had conducted the tests in a makeshift chemist's station.

"Well, there were pieces of wax, that's for sure. There were also tiny bits of candle wick in there as well. From that, I deduced that it might have been candle wax or something of that nature."

I pondered this. "Hmm… so it seems Venshlin dropped a candle on my dad, which then started the fire. If that's the case, his fingerprints would've melted away with the wax and burned with the material that was in the closet, and thereby hiding the evidence."

Alex was on top of his game. "I guess the plan imposed a light burden, huh?"

"Yeah," Shannon continued, for once ignoring Alex's humor. "And judging by the fact that there weren't any arsonist chemicals present, it seems that Venshlin didn't intend to burn down Wainwright."

"All the evidence would've been in the closet, and the only thing we recovered was an airplane training manual with all the pages torn out and a message written on the inside."

I presented Dr. Suzuki's findings on the card table near the rehearsal stage. Alex poured drinks (they were made more carefully to prevent a rerun of August 22) as everyone gathered to discuss Alex's findings.

"So, we've established that my dad was alive when the fire started, and that he had been taken to Wainwright during the early morning."

Alex studied the autopsy report. "You don't suppose he was put in a sleeping bag or something, do you?"

Zelda gently moved her cup in circles. "Why would you say that, Alex?"

"The extension cords that were found around his wrists show signs of having scraped a zipper; since he was wearing only boxers and a T-shirt, he didn't have a zipper anywhere on his person. That would indicate that he was put in a bag, maybe a sleeping bag, after being tied up."

Shannon reviewed the tests on the materials recovered. "A sleeping bag is typically made of polyester. And the tests do show polyester as having been present in the closet at the time of the fire."

"Polyester is also used in clothing, which I'm sure Dad was wearing at the time the fire started."

"I don't remember him wearing much material besides cotton; he does wear a jacket and tie during work, but that's the only thing he wears that isn't cotton."

"I had talked to him about my icicle dagger theory the night before the fire, and he wasn't wearing either."

"And there was too much polyester to account for even those. He was definitely in a sleeping bag with a metal zipper. I still don't understand who killed him, though."

"We might have to wait and see." I proceeded to round up everyone to head back to our houses. "Hopefully, we'll have answers before too long."

Four months passed, and no new evidence was found in either of the two murders. Rachel conducted an investigation on behalf of the police, but it quickly became clear that she was trying to incriminate me.

With the flow of time, normal events came and went as close to normal as circumstances allowed.

William York's murder trial started on October 23rd. It seemed like a normal trial, but William's attorney was Zachary Venshlin. I had reason to believe that the verdict would not be what it should be.

My 27th birthday came in November. Shannon, Zelda, and I had lunch at a Thai restaurant, and then Alex, Richard and I got together for a dinner of steak and ribs. The rest of the day went as normal.

By the time that Christmas came around (or Hanukkah in the case of Shannon and Zelda), the only evidence that the murders had taken place was the fact that Dad wasn't around. Normally, he would take the five of us gift shopping during the first week of December, but with him dead, we all bought each other black scarves.

Finally, on the third day of March, the murder trial of William York came to an end. As I predicted, the trial ended with a "not guilty" verdict for William York.

CHAPTER XI

Richard's Story

Richard Ralston here. I just wanted to write up a short story to add to a novel that Johnson is writing. You can skip ahead of this chapter and keep reading if you want, but I would highly recommend you stay and read this (especially if you're reading this for a class or whatnot).

Please note that what you are about to read is of graphic nature not suitable for younger audiences; reader discretion is advised. Per request of Zelda and Johnson, some details have been altered to minimize language.

The first thing I want to talk about is how much I hate living under someone else's authority. I tell you, the way those society-controlling bravos work, you'd think they'd only care to make themselves happy and not give a foxtrot about any other people in the world.

Another thing I hate is the high expectations from just about every important person life. I mean, seriously, of all the people you can't please, do they *have* to be the people that you have to please?

My type of life is a fast-paced kind of life. There are people whom I've met who have a desire to live like that. But they all have obstacles that get in the way of them acting out on that wish. Johnson thinks about consequences too carefully, and Rachel doesn't think carefully enough. You have to strike the perfect balance.

Ever since I was a kid, I've wanted to live life to my own standards and could care less about what others think. But as I grew older, my friends, parents, and my brother have told me that I would not be able to do that.

Despite what they said, I always tried to have the world suit my own wants. This, as you might expect, often led to a number of awkward moments, whether it be writing reports for school or watching a movie or all that jazz. Either way, my friends and I have hardly talked about those incidents.

My most frustrating episode was when I was trying to get my driver's license. I had to retake the driving exam twelve times because of me flunking the maneuverability test.

And yes, I know that there's the old saying "You can be happy now or you can be happy later, but you can't have both." Most people would choose to be happy later, but that's because most people haven't had their lives shattered by a plane crash.

As I'm sure you already know, Johnson and his family were involved in the crash of Firebird Airlines Flight 934, and his brother had been killed in that crash. And you know that the mechanic who serviced the plane before the accident took the blame for the airline's mistake.

I knew then that the end could not be foreseen at all, and that one should take advantage of what they have. If they wait until tomorrow to be happy, they would never be happy at all because there won't be a tomorrow.

I could go on a ramble about how much I had become embittered by the events of that crash, but Johnson has asked that I be as brief as possible.

Since no one has explained the trial of Firebird Airlines, I have taken it upon myself to do so.

My girlfriend's sister, Zelda, had followed the NTSB in their investigation into the crash. She had also learned from the CEO of Firebird that the airline had a history of incidents that came about from poor maintenance.

She sent the information to the newspapers, and it made front page news across the country.

As I read the Enquirer's article about Zelda's discovery, the news showed many grieving relatives and friends who had filed a lawsuit against Firebird Airlines. I was thinking about how much it would suck to be Firebird Airlines, and that there was no hope of them getting out of this mess.

But what happened in the end was bittersweet in that it made me re-evaluate my life, but I was saddened that justice was not served.

Rachel Dinesen was my girlfriend in high school. She had the same rebellious tendencies as I did, and I could tell she wanted our relationship to last. To prove how much she wanted me, she sang a song at prom that had me get made fun of by my peers for a month. Of course, I was able to live with it for the time being.

We used to hang out in high school, when I was more rebellious than I am now. She would listen to songs that could have gotten her expelled, she had tattoos and body piercings; you would never have even envisaged that she would've been able to get into the police force.

Zelda told me that Rachel was a bad influence and that I should break up with her. Now, Zelda and I have locked antlers with each other a lot, mainly because we hold different views about our consciences.

Zelda takes everything way too seriously and always plays by the rules. I tend to believe it's because she's Jewish (I have nothing against Jews, though; in fact, I don't understand why anti-Semitism even exists at all) though she claims she has learned from other people's mistakes as opposed to making her own mistakes.

Even when she's relaxed and at home, she still wears her police uniform and doesn't surf the Internet, and she feels satisfied with life.

In my opinion, life should be about having as much fun as possible. And I often believe that with the great expectations from life, a satisfying identity comes before an honest identity. So, while I do get to enjoy a fulfilling career as a professional baseball player, I think that one shouldn't have to conform to others just because "it's the correct thing to do."

But while I'm not happy about strict rules, I do follow rules to some degree. The only thing I have a problem with is conforming to expectations.

It was when I was in college, the week after the Firebird Airlines trial, when I broke up with Rachel.

I was in my physics class watching a presentation from another student; he was lecturing on how an airplane could lose its nose in flight and then fly upward for an extra few seconds before plummeting to Earth. Shannon was also present, but she was having a hard time focusing.

I secretly wrote a note to her. "Hey, Shannon. Have you been handling yourself okay?"

She wrote a long note to explain what happened at the Firebird Airlines lawsuit trial, which resulted in a "not guilty" verdict in favor of Firebird Airlines.

Representing Firebird Airlines was Harold Satchel. He was the most legendary defense attorney in the whole state of Ohio. But with him representing an airline that was dancing with the Devil, he could very well have been surrounded by a ring of flamethrowers.

You'd think that with Zelda's thorough report in the newspaper that the case would have been open and shut in less than 30 seconds.

But Zelda didn't realize that the evidence was obtained as part of the criminal investigation without a warrant. It was thus rendered unusable.

Furthermore, the ATC tape with the post-crash distress message, which was not mentioned in Zelda's report, contained evidence that confirmed the cause of the accident as being poor maintenance.

The mechanic who supervised the maintenance work admitted to putting a bent rivet in the fin despite knowing it was not up to the job. He was found guilty of negligence and was terminated the following day.

Rachel came to my dorm the following day to give me a birthday present. She always gave me a present every year as a token of our boyfriend-girlfriend relationship; my birthday "happened" once every four years. My birthday didn't actually "happen" on that particular year.

I had told her about the crash the day after it happened, and she laughed in my face; she thought that it was a publicity stunt since the damage to the plane did not damage the radio.

Shannon was shattered that Terrence did not survive the crash, but that piece of news made Rachel laugh even harder.

And I might as well have been Alex when I mentioned the outcome of the trial that followed.

With that, I threw the unopened present out the window of my dorm room and pushed her out the door.

"I should've listened to Zelda." With that, I slammed the door in her face.

I still haven't regretted my decision to start going out with Shannon. I've been by her side in times of trouble, and she's helped me with getting a grip on my emotions.

I eventually found that dumping Rachel and going out with Shannon had saved her life; she was close to committing suicide because of Terrence's death. I was able to inspire her to cherish her own life and not let herself get beat down by the harsh reality of life.

Rachel was deeply exasperated about me dumping her for her callousness about Firebird Airlines Flight 934. I half-expected her to start calling me "Dick" afterward, but she went on calling me "Rickey" as a reference to the incident at prom.

But I stood by my decision to forsake her. If she was going to laugh at other people suffering or dying, like hotel she would be staying with me. I'm sure Shannon was grateful for my choice to leave Rachel and take up being with her.

I'm surprised that Johnson had not found out about Rachel's secret flaws until after the fire at Wainwright.

Chapter XII

Trial of Error

No one had been prepared for the verdict that had been delivered at the trial.

"How the hotel was William found not guilty?" Patrick tugged on the flaps of his jacket and flopped himself into the booth at the nearby diner.

I sat down next to Shannon and Zelda. "I would say that his replacement attorney was the reason."

Richard sat next to his brother followed by Alex. "You think so?"

"Well, yeah. I have strong reason to suspect him for the murders of Satchel and my father. And from the way that he managed to get his client acquitted, he may have something to do with all these past court cases."

Shannon looked up from the menu. "Did anyone else feel a sense of fear looking at him?"

Alex adjusted his glasses. "What do you mean?"

"Well, his face was really tight, and his eyebrows were thick, and that black hair looked like it was dripping sideways. Plus, his clothes appeared to be some shade of red."

"You mean they weren't brown?"

"One might be tempted to think they were brown, but I am sure they were red."

Zelda thought back to her memory of Venshlin in the courtroom. "Yeah. And the way he walked, you'd think there were sycamore seed pods in his left shoe."

I reached for the note we found at the apartment. "Well, the note does mention a broken shin."

That's when the waitress came over. "Are you all ready to order?"

Everyone placed their order, and after the waitress left, we resumed our discussion.

Shannon ran her fingers through her blonde hair. "It's especially disturbing that the defense attorney was almost the exact opposite of the DA."

"Yeah." Alex straightened his bowtie. "Mr. McCrery is probably old enough to be Venshlin's father."

The waitress returned with our drinks. "Your food will be here shortly."

I took a sip from my hot chocolate. "Yeah, McCrery's thick beard and gray hair and gnarled fingers…"

"And his Dutch accent." Patrick was stirring his coffee. "That was what struck me as noticeable."

"What about Judge Hershel? He looked as though he had known William before the trial."

"Why would you say that, Johnson?"

"Usually, judges are supposed to observe the case from a completely objective view; Judge Hershel seemed to show a sign of having done something against William in the past."

Richard took the cherry off the top of his milkshake. "Is that why William York had been found not guilty?"

Zelda rubbed her chin. "No, there were two theories as to why the airbag ended up in the microwave. The first one was that William had tried to kill his father to collect an insurance claim on him."

"Scott had told me that William had been fired a few years back." Patrick grabbed a creamer from the saucer. "I was there to rewrite the policy on Scott before William could kill him for the money."

Alex swallowed a swig of his drink. "Venshlin claimed that Scott himself had tried to kill his son out of fear of that exact scenario taking place, but in doing so, he had unwittingly allowed the opposite to happen without William having any idea what had happened."

"Both sides had convincing arguments," Shannon drew lines in the water drops on her glass, "and the evidence pointed in both directions. They couldn't prove what gloves were used in removing the car's airbag."

"I guess that's why they had to call in a psychologist to settle the dispute." Alex exhaled a barely audible laugh.

Richard stuck his straw in his shake. "I think it had to do with something Venshlin had said in the courtroom."

Patrick remembered the attorney's words verbatim, and he spoke with a tone filled with ersatz authority. "'If one must live, one must learn. If one must learn, one must be willing to progress at any time. Otherwise, they will forever be blinded by the light which they refuse to see.'"

I shook my head. "So, he managed to sway the jury by claiming that the conclusion of William York having been the one to cause his father's death was too easy to come to."

"Yeah." Alex shrugged. "Imagine if someone had made that statement about PSA Flight 1771."

"Can you please not bring that up?" Shannon moaned.

"Oh, right. I forgot your grandfather was on that flight."

"How could you have forgotten? He was the intended victim of that crash, for golf's sake!"

The waitress came by with our meals and laid out each of the dishes in front of each of us six.

I hastened to get the conversation back on subject. "So, Patrick, how did the airbag get to the microwave?"

Patrick took a sip from his coffee. "Well, when I got to the York house, William and his father Scott were both there. I was there, as you know, to rewrite Scott's insurance policy so that William York would not be the beneficiary."

"Why?"

"William had been fired years ago, and Scott suspected that William would try to kill him to collect his insurance. He wanted his life insurance policy rewritten to benefit William's brother, Michael, before William did try to kill him."

"So, what happened after you arrived?"

"Scott and I sat down at the dining room table to start the rewrite. While we did that, William went to the kitchen to, as he claimed, get something to eat."

"What was he actually doing?"

"He went to the fridge to get what Scott and I thought was a tray of leftover lasagna. In actuality, it was an airbag, which William had removed from his car and disguised as a tray of lasagna."

"What happened next?"

"William stuck the airbag in the microwave, started it, and went back to the fridge so that he could use the door as a shield from the explosion that followed. The shrapnel flew at me and Scott at high speed. Scott was hit and killed, but I was untouched."

"What did William do afterward?"

"He looked around the fridge door to see the damage he had caused. We both saw a deployed airbag dangling from the hollow piece of metal that used to be a microwave, surrounded by a fine white powder. I ran out the back door before William could do anything more."

"William admitted that the job from which he was fired was that of a mechanic. That would give him the expertise to remove an airbag from a car."

"Yeah, but Venshlin said that Scott had asked William to remove the airbag. Since Scott's dead, and the only one that could confirm that assertion was William (which he did), there wasn't any firm answer as to whether or not that was true."

"Especially since there were two opposing but equally supportable theories as to how Scott was killed."

Alex took a bite from his cheese omelet. "Does anyone think that Scott would've been scared enough to have tried to kill his son out of paranoia?"

Richard squeezed his sandwich together. "I know that that could not have happened."

I just slowly stirred my soup. "Well, if Venshlin hadn't made such a convincing argument, the jury certainly would not have come to the decision they came to."

Zelda tapped her fingers together. "Venshlin had made the case that life insurance was a common motive for murder."

Patrick nodded. "That does appear to be a fairly wide trend, murders committed by family members under a great deal of financial stress. And surely, William was under such a great amount of financial stress."

Richard forced his knife through his steak in one clean cut. "That's certainly enough of a motive for William to have killed his father."

"Venshlin says that that psychology was what prompted Scott to believe that he had to kill William in order to save his own life."

Richard glared at me. "Why are you making arguments for the defense? You know that that charlie story is nothing but a mike-foxtrotting pile of bravo-sierra!"

Shannon grabbed his wrist. "I will not have you talking like that, Richard!"

Alex turned to the waitress. "Check, please."

Zelda and I got boxes for our meals and went out to the cruiser, leaving Richard and Shannon alone at the table.

Outside, the three of us had had a brief discussion.

"I have got to find out more about this Venshlin guy."

"Well, we don't know where he is or where he could be at the moment."

"The only thing we know for sure is that he had studied at the Wainwright Law Academy. But we can't go there to investigate; that place is still being repaired from the fire there in October."

That's when a memory crossed my mind. "Hey, wait a second. I just remembered something."

Zelda looked to me. "Yeah? What?"

"During my meeting with Satchel, he mentioned that Venshlin had been hired at the law firm the day before."

Alex nodded. "I guess that explains how he managed to get chosen as William's attorney so quickly."

"So that must mean that he's got his own office over at Landenberg by now. I'll take a look there this evening."

"Alright." Alex stepped into his van. "Good luck."

Alex stayed behind to wait for Richard and Shannon, and Zelda and I drove off.

Then, as we drove away from the diner, another thought crossed my mind. "Wait… Venshlin had been chosen for the case as a new hire."

"What's your point?"

"Something just doesn't add up. First of all, why did William choose an attorney without any experience at all? And how did said attorney manage to win the case?"

"You probably already have an answer to the second question; though he didn't seem to have time to study the case between Satchel's murder and the start of the trial."

"Unless… did he manage to orchestrate the events so as to have him representing William?"

Chapter XIII

Zachary Venshlin

When I found Venshlin's office, it looked just like what you'd expect a lawyer's office to look like. Everything was in a perfect array of papers and files, and you could tell that they had been here for a few months. And on the wall next to the window, there was a diploma from Wainwright Law Academy in a stained cherry wood frame.

Venshlin was nowhere to be seen, so I decided to take an intrepid gamble and trawl the office for clues. Since I was a "private eye," I didn't feel the need for a search warrant, as I wasn't an "official" investigator.

I opened the top drawer of Venshlin's desk and found a peculiar assortment of items. There were tiny plastic bags of green and orange sugar crystals, and a small makeup kit. I also found a bottle of nail polish, nail polish remover, a curling iron, and some hairbands.

If this wasn't Weirdsville, I didn't know what was.

The file cabinet also had some interesting information. There were court cases which I could tell Venshlin had read about and studied minutely. Paragraphs and sentences were highlighted and underlined, and notes had been written in the margins of the pages in each report.

For some reason, I had an entrenched notion that I had seen the handwriting somewhere before.

There was one report in particular which seemed to be very interesting to Venshlin. It was a report about the Firebird Airlines trial. Now, there was a potential lead.

I could see that Venshlin was examining errors with the trial about Flight 934. He had written notes about evidence that contributed to the ultimate outcome, the most tantalizing being my distress call from the crashed plane to air traffic control.

But there was another question raised by the report.

Why would Venshlin be studying this particular case?

Venshlin was still logged onto his computer, and I saw that he had been typing a research report on the attorneys involved in the Firebird trial, as well as others that followed.

There was a note about the mechanic who supervised the maintenance carried out on the plane before the crash. (The name had been blacked out.) He had appealed to the NTSB to get his license back, but he was unsuccessful.

I printed out a copy of this document for myself and went back to the file cabinet.

I was already suspicious that Venshlin had killed my father. Now I knew that for a fact. I also had reason to suspect that he was sabotaging these court cases. Now I needed to find out why.

As I trawled through the records, I could see that there was a stack of files about each of the bad trials. Upon further investigation, I could see that Satchel had indeed served in a number of the bad trials.

And Satchel had served as the defense attorney in the Firebird Airlines trial. That seemed to be a breakthrough right there in the office.

And judging from Dad's death, it seemed evident that Venshlin was indeed cognizant with how good a detective my father was.

That's when I remembered the poem I had found back at Wainwright.

"Is this the end? I'm afraid not [...] But there is still business left that's unfinished / I must now wait 'til the chase has diminished"

I realized that the story was far from over. I needed to know what the next chapter was.

I grabbed the document I had printed from the printer, and a note slipped out of the packet and landed on the floor. I picked it up and unfolded it.

And lo and behold, there was another poem.

Had enough? Ha! I have yet to be through
Even now, I am not finished with you
Rest assured judgment is on its way
So, keep in mind what I did say
Horror and dread around
Every bend
Learning your life is nearing its end

10, 26, 5, 7, 15, 20, 28

The note made me wonder if Venshlin predicted that I would come to his office and investigate. But I knew now that I was personally involved now.

I folded the note and put it with the other two notes I had. Then I wrote down everything I had found in my notepad, took a few of the bags of crystals from the desk drawer, and gathered all of the documents I found into a neat pile. I then put everything into plastic bags and headed to the subway to report my findings to the rest of the gang.

When I got to the station, I saw a number of people walking out of a train tunnel. Some were grumbling, but others seemed to have been struck by fear. A few were talking to the station patrollers.

Once again, my insuppressible curiosity brought me to the crowd stepping off the side-walkway. As I walked to them, I counted the people on the platform; 104 in total.

"Hey, what's going on over here?"

A young woman walked up to me. "There's a train that got stuck in that tunnel. We were told to get off and head down the walkway to the station."

I scratched my ear. "What happened?"

"The train must have hit something, and it got stuck in one of the axles. At least, that's what I think happened."

"Hm. Is the train still there?"

"Yes, it is."

"I'm going to go take a look at that." I made my way to the walkway running along the track and headed down the tunnel to the train.

It was about forty minutes of walking before I saw the train. The tunnel was too dark to make out much; the only light was coming from inside the train. That light wasn't being cast upon the tracks on which the train stood, so I had to use my flashlight to see what had caused the train to stop.

When I turned it on, I almost wanted to turn it back off.

There was a long trail of blood streaks trailing down the track. From the trail, I could deduce that the train was going away from the station I had come from when it hit someone.

I followed the trail away from the train and found that it ended about 40 feet from the rear of the train. I could tell that the train was going pretty fast at the time of the impact.

There was also a bloody dent on the third rail, which indicated that the victim had either jumped off the walkway or was pushed off. If they had hit the third rail, they would've been electrocuted pretty much instantaneously. So, they could not have been alive when they were hit.

I lowered myself onto the track below to examine the train's undercarriage, being careful not to step in any of the blood on the cement.

From what I could see from that position, the back of the train was completely intact. I noticed that the brakes had not been engaged, and from that angle I saw no damage that could have contributed to the train being stopped.

I photographed the blood patterns near the dent in the third rail and the state of the back end of the train, climbed back up to the walkway, and walked down the catwalk to assay the other end of the train.

As I walked along the side of the train, I could see that the passenger area of all eight cars of the train appeared to be perfectly intact. But from what I was told, the undercarriage must have been damaged enough to stop the train. Using my walking to measure the length of one of the coaches, I found the length of each car to be 20 feet long.

So, from the moment the train hit the body on the track, the damage slowed the train to a stop over a 200-foot length of the track. I would need to calculate the train's weight in order to determine how fast the train was moving when the accident occurred.

I approached the front of the train expecting the worst.

At the front of the train, there wasn't any damage to the front buffers at all. So, whoever got hit wasn't standing at the time of impact.

I went down onto the track to examine the underside of the train. The axles and brakes on this end of the train were mangled. Bloody shreds of flesh and various materials were tangled in the warped metal; the state of the damage would've prevented the train from moving any further. I started taking pictures of the damage.

This finding, as well as witness testimony from before I went into the tunnel, led me to the conclusion that something (or someone) must have been hit by the train.

Based on the presence of what appeared to be human tissue, it seemed like it was some*one*.

A question suddenly came to my mind at that moment.

How did they get here in the first place? They could not have been on board the train, or else it wouldn't have stopped. And if they were attempting to commit suicide, why take a long walk down the tunnel before jumping onto the track? The emergency exit near the start of the blood trail couldn't be used by just anyone. And they didn't jump as the train was coming in through the tunnel since there was no damage at all to the train's buffers, as well as a large puddle of blood under the third rail.

The only way they could have ended up here was if they were taken here forcefully. I realized there was only one thing that could have led this to happen.

This was no accident; this was murder.

And from the poem I found in Venshlin's office, I knew exactly who it was and who killed him.

CHAPTER XIV

Murder #3

I raced down the tunnel toward the station I had been on my way to before the gruesome discovery. I was both scared for my life and eager to share my discoveries with the rest of the gang.

I was exhausted after an hour of running. When I made it to the station, I could see Rachel and her team heading to the tunnel I had come from. She caught sight of me and sprinted in my direction.

"Well well well, what brings you here tonight, Vasquez Private Eye?"

"There's been a third murder."

"Oh, you've heard the rumor, too, hmm?"

"It's true. If you're willing to take the long walk down the tunnel, go right ahead."

"What do you mean?"

"Judge Hershel got thrown onto the tracks and was run over by a train."

"You mean the judge that presided over the murder trial yesterday?"

"Yeah, that was him."

"And how do you know that?"

"I did some trawling at the law firm earlier today and found a suspect for these crimes."

"Yeah? Who?"

"Zachary Venshlin."

Rachel knew who I was talking about. "Wasn't he the defense attorney for that trial?"

"Yes, he was. I have good reason to believe that he was also the one wreaking havoc with the justice system."

"You don't say? So, what did you find out about your friend Zachary Venshlin?"

I cleared my throat. "I did find a treasure of information about his background. He had graduated from Wainwright Law Academy last year, and he took a job at the Landenberg firm four months ago. He served in his first trial defending William York yesterday.

"From what I found, he seemed to be studying court cases from all the way back to the trial of Firebird Airlines. You remember that, right?"

She snickered. "Yeah, I remember that. I'm amazed at how badly that case turned out."

"Yeah. Anyway, I found this note which indicated that Venshlin was planning to kill Hershel. He has already killed Satchel and my dad, (the latter being the reason for me being a 'private eye' in this investigation) and I do believe that he had killed Hershel as well."

"You don't say?" Rachel adjusted her hat and started for the tunnel. "I'm watching you, Vasquez Private Eye."

I knew I had wound up in the wrong place at the wrong time, and Rachel was bound to grasp that detail and exploit it for her own gain. I continued up to the street and regrouped the others to share my new info.

My friends and I gathered for dinner that evening, and I told them about what I found at Venshlin's office.

They each read the documents I had swiped, with Zelda noting all the parts that Venshlin had highlighted as well as his margin notes.

Richard adjusted his hat. "So, what else did you find at Landenberg, Johnson?"

"In Venshlin's desk drawer, there were what appeared to be makeup accessories."

"Makeup? You mean like lipstick, eye liner, nail polish, facial cream, and stuff like that?"

"Yeah. I have no idea why he has those."

Alex was quick to interject. "Maybe he has a girlfriend and he's holding her stuff."

Shannon turned a hard glare that spelled out "You can't be serious" while Zelda wrote the information in her notepad.

"I also found little bags of what looked like green and orange sugar in the drawer." I took a sip from my hot chocolate as they pondered the information.

"Wait a minute." Shannon looked at me. "Did you say you found little packets of green and orange sugar?"

"Yes, I did." I took out the packets I had taken and gave them to her. "I wasn't sure what they were exactly, so I took a few packets for you to test."

Shannon seized them from my hand as soon as I opened it. "I know what this is!"

Alex recognized it as well. "Isn't that the drink-mix that you made which led to my secret life?"

Richard confirmed to him. "Yes, it is."

Shannon stood up. "I need to talk to Johnson… alone."

I was confused, but there was an ominous tone in her rasping voice. "Why can't you just talk to me right here?"

Shannon didn't answer; she just grabbed my shoulder and led me outside the diner.

We went around to the back of the building outside the employee's entrance.

"So, what are we doing here, Shannon?"

"Shhh! Keep your voice down!"

She looked around to make sure that we were the only people present.

She took a hard swallow and turned to me. "Um… I've been meaning to tell you something, Johnson."

"Yeah? What?"

"I think I'm being blackmailed."

"What do you mean?"

"I can't explain right now. But I wrote an entry in my journal that explains it."

"Can't you explain at least some of it right now?"

Shannon was wringing her hands nervously. "I wish I could, but I'm worried that the blackmailer is watching us right now. And I have no idea who it us or what they can do."

"Well, I already told you that I found those packets in Venshlin's office."

"So, what do you think that means, detective boy?"

I was surprised by her snappish response. "Would it not mean that Venshlin is blackmailing you?"

"Of course not. It means that Zachary Venshlin is not a real person!"

"We all saw him in the courtroom."

"No, I don't mean in that sense; I mean that someone is disguising themselves using my drugs, and they're going under the pseudonym Zachary Venshlin."

"Okay. So, we just need to find out who he really is and prove them guilty of the murders."

"But if we don't know who Venshlin really is, how are we supposed to know what we're really up against?"

"That's what I'm trying to find out."

"But that note you and my sister found at Wainwright seemed to be indicating that you won't want the answer to this mystery. I'm very concerned that something abysmal is sure to happen here."

"Come on, Shannon; that's just the reaction-to-Firebird-934 part of your mind talking."

Shannon appeared to be offended. "How can you be so blasé about a crash that killed your brother?"

It was at that time that the others came over to check on us. "What are you guys doing here?"

Shannon scrambled to her feet. "Nothing."

Alex cracked a smile. "Sure, it was nothing."

Zelda led us back to the parking lot. "It's starting to get late; we should probably head home."

Alex opened the cruiser door for Richard and Shannon. "Well, I'm going over to my store. You can take Richard and Johnson to their places on your girls' way home."

As he turned to his van, I got in next to Zelda. "Before I go home, Shannon wanted to give me something at your place. So, do you think I could stop there really quick?"

Zelda started the engine. "Yeah, I can do that."

As soon as Zelda put the cruiser in park, Shannon was the first one out of the vehicle. She jumped up the porch steps and then disappeared into the door.

Zelda seemed confused as she unbuckled herself and took the keys from the ignition. She climbed out, walked to the front door, and nearly got run over by Shannon as she sprinted back out.

Shannon returned with an envelope and looked at me with panicked eyes. "Johnson, I'm holding my trust to you that you will not share this entry with anyone."

After a moment's worth of paralyzed disinclination, I appropriated the envelope. "So, can you tell me what it's about right now, or...?"

"I wish I could, but I dare not speak further for fear that Venshlin is close by."

She spun around on her heel and returned to the house, leaving me holding the envelope. From the way she spoke, I should've been scared for my life. But I instead felt a curious confusion as to what there was to fear.

Zelda got back in the cruiser to take me home. "What's that she gave you?"

"I wish I could tell you. But at the moment, I think that Shannon wants me to keep a secret."

"Why would that be?"

"I have no idea. She said she thought Zachary Venshlin was a pseudonym."

"Yeah?"

"Judging from what she told me, it might be an excerpt from her journal."

"What exactly is she trying to tell you?"

"Well, there's only one way to find out." I tore open the sealed flap and withdrew the contents...

CHAPTER XV

Shannon's Story

I'd like to at this time discuss a few important facts regarding what you've read in Johnson's novel (or to be more precise, Alex's chapter *in* Johnson's novel.).

You've likely read about the drink mix I had made that caused Alex's Jekyll-and-Hyde duality, (or as Alex called it, his "Chuckle-and-Chide" duality.) and so I thought I'd go into more detail on that.

The following is an excerpt from my journal from the week of August 31st, 20—.

On the night of August 22nd, 20—, six months after the acquittal of Firebird Airlines from its role in the crash of Flight 934, I received a package of chemicals that I had ordered over the internet.

My friends have reputed me as a nervous wreck after I was nearly run over by a car as a kid. (Johnson already told you that story.) I was shaken by the event, and what made it more disconcerting was that Johnson was inspired to be a policeman because of it. And my sister joining him as well? What am I, chopped liver?

Johnson's brother, Terrence, was the only person who had taken the time to understand my pain. His death left a festering wound that was salted after the demons at Firebird Airlines were acquitted of the charges laid on them.

Alex was such an idiotic clown, and I found him to be unbearable. He never stops telling jokes, and he was in every way slap happy. I wanted to be more courageous so I could get past the loss of my best friend.

So, on the night of August 22nd, Alex invited all of us to Dr. Chuckle's Prank Lab and Gag Shop. I knew about the drink station in the basement, so I decided to try out my new batch of chemicals and find a way to put an end to all of my troubles once and for all.

The basement was a simple room with concrete walls and a wood framework ceiling with fiberglass insulation. Dust and cobwebs covered the wooden crates scattered around the area, and a single bare light bulb hanging above the staircase door was the only light source in the room.

Alex and the others were practicing a comedy routine, and I was at work at the drink lab conducting experiments with my new chemicals.

Using light from a Bunsen burner, I sought to find a way to toughen up my personality and destroy what my friends and Alex called my "paranoia." My boyfriend, Richard, had mentioned that some of Alex's drinks could provoke unusual behaviors, (similar to alcohol, but without the after effects) so I decided to utilize those in my experiments.

After sixty-three experiments, I finally had it ready. I wrote down the recipe, and there only existed the last step of putting my creation to the test.

I asked Richard to make a batch of punch for all of us, and he complied. But what no one realized was that he had mistakenly taken my vial to add to the punch.

I had planned to slip the mix into Alex's drink, but for the reason above, I wasn't able to do that. But I decided to go with the cover plan.

I wanted the airline to face the justice they deserve, and I proposed a toast to finding a way to get that to happen.

We agreed and downed the punch in one gulp.

It's still too distressing to this day to fully put on paper what happened next. All I can say is that we transformed into beings that reflected our deepest, darkest desires.

Following the incident, we started transforming into our shadow forms by night every night. I soon found that we had received such a large dose of the mix from the original batch of tainted punch that we effectively became werewolves.

Within weeks, it became evident that we were starting to lose a foothold on our true state of mind. That was when it occurred to me that if we were to be our normal selves, I had to find an antidote, and fast.

I studied the recipe for my original crystal mix to find a list of ingredients to counteract the effects. It was five weeks before I found the antidote. But the aura was uncertain; some of us actually liked to live as their secret side, particularly Alex. When the brew was mixed and dispensed, we just stood with indecision staring at the glasses of bubbling pink punch.

It was eight minutes before we managed to pick up the cups. Alex put his back on the table, but the rest of us were able to drink off the punch.

Before long, all of us were as average as you would ever believe us to be.

Since Alex never consumed the antidote, he remained a dual-faced being; a sick, geeky clown by day, and a hardened bounty hunter by night.

I found myself to be particularly fond of Alex's tougher self, who addressed himself as Brandon Chide. (Though I still wonder if Alex's real side had chosen that name.)

The ordeal taught me an important lesson: the world is no place for a coward, but it's better to live as a coward than to die as a soldier.

Following the discovery and recovery of my unheard-of experiments, I thought that I would be able to forget about the bizarre incident.

Not even 3 = 5 could have been more wrong.

Less than a week later, I received mysterious packages on my doorstep. They all had the chemicals I had used to create my potions that accursed night.

At first, I thought that they were delivered to the wrong address, as I was not placing out any orders for any of what I was receiving. This proved incorrect when I looked at the address sticker on each box and found that they presented the name of Shannon Edith Amanda Thomson.

I was able to discern from the packages that someone knew about my serums. Since I was the only one who knew the recipe, they were sending me the ingredients needed to make the potions. But if that was the case, there were three questions which I had to answer:

How did they find out which potions to send me? Who wanted it? And what did they want with it?

There was a message taped to the side of the biggest of the boxes. I peeled back the tape which held the white bulging envelope to the cardboard box and studied its exterior. When I saw nothing unusual, I fished out a letter opener and wedged it under the sealed flap.

The envelope was stuffed with tiny plastic pouches and a black piece of paper. When I unfolded it, my suspicions were confirmed; there was a typed poem written in red pastel.

> What a surprise is at your front door
> And just what is it I'm desperate for?
> I could tell you, but then you'd have to die
> Now read this carefully and don't ask why
> With these liquors concoct your brews
> Reject these orders and it's the big snooze
> I know where you live and who you are
> Get it all made and drive in your car
> Have a look at the code word in this note
> That's where you'll take them. Make haste to the cote

When I finished, I thought about calling the police. But I didn't know who wrote it, and I knew that I could be playing Russian roulette if I had called the police, so I decided against doing so.

I moved all the boxes to my lab in the basement and took out my glassware from the cabinet. I unpacked the boxes and laid the contents across the counter.

I measured out the proper amount of each chemical in calibrated beakers, and then poured each into a flask. I turned on one of the Bunsen burners and placed the glowing purple liquid over the flame.

When all the liquid had boiled away, all that was left was 50 grams of neon green powder. This was the first phase of transformation.

I had also received shipments of ingredients for the antidote mixture, so the blackmailer likely wanted that as well. So again, I measured out the ingredients, mixed them together, and boiled the bleached yellow serum until I was left with 50 grams of orange powder.

The mixture was dispensed in the small plastic bags in dose-sized amounts, and I put them in a large plastic bag. Then I picked up the note that came with the bags and tried to figure out where I was supposed to go.

I managed to discern the destination to be Wainwright Law Academy.

It was 2 AM when I left for Wainwright. I wasn't sure who I was dealing with, and so I spent 15 minutes sitting at the wheel of my car without moving before I started up the engine to drive to Wainwright. When I reached Wainwright, I almost fell asleep when I shut off the engine. I was only awoken when someone started knocking on my door.

I looked out the window, and saw a figure clad in black. They had a scarf wrapped around their head to hide their face, sunglasses concealing the eyes, and they wore a fedora to hide their hair.

I hesitantly rolled down the window. "A-Are y-you the p-person I'm supposed to meet?"

They looked at me and said nothing. I reached for the glove compartment, and I took out the bags which contained the sugars I had made. They signaled for me to give it to them, which I complied.

I reached for the key to start the engine back up. "I'm going to go now."

A gloved hand clasped my shoulder, and they made a gesture for me to get out of the car. They signaled for me to follow them down a dark alley next to the building. I was becoming more and more frightened by the minute.

They led me to a secluded spot behind a dumpster and removed a brick from the wall. They pointed to me, showed me the bags of drink mix I had given them, and put a few into the cavity where the brick was.

"You want me to put the bags into this cavity when I bring them here?"

They nodded, took the bags out, replaced the brick, and drew an X on the brick with blue chalk.

I looked back toward the car, half hoping for Chide to come by and rescue me.

When I turned back around to look at the mysterious figure again, they were gone.

CHAPTER XVI

Train of Thought

Teams spent nearly a week cleaning up the debris from under the ruined train. Small parts of the train had come loose, causing tiny specs of metal to become intermingled with body parts and the various materials sucked under the train.

The process was time consuming and meticulous. But they were able to collect all the fabric, body parts, and debris that didn't belong to the train, which was sent to Dr. Suzuki for analysis.

The examination station was practically a slaughtering block. Shannon did have hemophobia, and the remains of what I suspected was Judge Hershel's body nearly made her vomit.

Dr. Suzuki was in a baffled state. "How am I supposed to sort out this mess?"

Zelda and I were busy painstakingly sorting out the tiny fragments from the scene of the crime.

The only recovered debris that was remotely intact were buttons from pants, a shirt, and a jacket, a one-inch square of polyester from a green necktie, a pair of black leather shoes with the feet still inside, zipper teeth, and extension cord plugs, all of which were covered in blood.

The recognizable body parts were fingers, feet, limbs that were stripped to the bone, a head with the face shredded beyond recognition, a severed jaw with all of the teeth still embedded within, a torso with exposed and cracked ribs, and a part of the lower body region that confirmed the gender of the victim as a male.

Everything else that was found was thousands of shreds the size of pencil shavings.

DNA samples were extracted from the pieces of tissue and recovered blood to confirm that all the tissue was the same person. All the intact body parts were laid out on the table like a giant puzzle.

The other recovered material was sorted out in another pile. There were numerous bits of cotton, linen, and polyester, which must have been pieces of clothing. Other materials that were recovered seemed to be copper wire and extension cord insulation material.

Shannon was lifting up fingerprints from the recovered fingers. "How on earth do you create this kind of damage by just running a train over the victim?"

"Judging by the fact that hardly any whole body parts were recovered, it would seem that the victim had died long before they were hit by the train."

"You would think the body had started to decay when the victim was hit?"

"Precisely."

While Shannon was busy comparing teeth, bones, and fingerprints from the victim to dental, X-ray, and fingerprint records of numerous people in the area, Zelda and I tried to work out how the train interacted with the victim, and whether it would be enough to completely obliterate a human body.

"I did notice a dent in the third rail about 200 feet from where the train's front buffer stopped, and the brakes had not been engaged prior to the train stopping. I think there were 104 people on the train; I saw them walking into the station from the tunnel where the scene was."

Shannon was taking blood samples from the intact body parts to run toxicology tests. "Do you remember off the top of your head the distribution of men, women, and children on the train? And how long the train was?"

I strained to remember. "There were eight coaches that made up the train. I'm not sure how many people there were, but I believe there were... 20 kids, 37 women, and 47 men. It may or may not be exactly right."

Zelda hurried to write the numbers in her notepad. She used those to calculate the train's weight, and from there, the speed at the time of impact. Those numbers would be used to see just how much time had passed between death and impact.

In the meantime, I examined the toxicology test results. All the analyses found nothing to suggest the victim was drunk or drugged at any time before or after death.

Dr. Suzuki wasn't entirely sure if the victim had any preexisting injuries before being killed, as the damage from the train impact would've likely hidden any wounds that existed prior to being hit by the train.

The DNA tests came back, and we were able to confirm that all the body parts were from one person. The samples were compared to DNA profiles of people throughout the area.

Then, the search turned up matches to the teeth, bones, and fingerprints of the victim.

The results of all of the tests confirmed that the victim on the tracks was Justice Martin James Hershel.

We met back up with the other three in the basement of Alex's store to discuss what we found in Dr. Suzuki's office.

"So, now we know that Hershel is dead." Shannon was over at the drink station. "Now, we need to figure out how he was killed."

Richard was examining the subway schedule to figure out when Hershel could've landed on the track. "The incident happened toward one end of a shuttle track, so there would've only been one train on the line."

"From the blood patterns, it would appear the train was heading toward the closer end; so, there was much more time to dispose of him before he was run over."

"But how did he get there?"

Zelda had managed to figure out the train's speed when it hit Hershel. "There were bits of extension cord found under the train, so it would seem likely that he was tied and gagged, then brought to the dump site."

I look at the subway schedule for today to see when the train could've passed by. "So, how could Venshlin have gotten Hershel to the tunnel without being noticed? He would need a key to use the emergency exit tunnel."

"He was able to abduct and kill Satchel in the subway without detection, and he managed to set a fire in Wainwright."

"But that's still doesn't answer the essential question of why he was killed."

Alex looked at one of the botched case files. "One case that ended with a bad verdict was a kidnapping case by one of the rail company's workers, so Venshlin could've gotten a key for the emergency exit that way."

"He must've put a lot of thought into his plan, then."

Shannon thought back to what I had said about Hershel yesterday. "Didn't you think that Hershel knew William before the trial?"

"Yeah, I did."

"I wonder why."

"How about we take another look at the documents that I got from Venshlin's office?"

Richard had put them in a box; he retrieved them from under the drink station counter where Shannon was working.

I sifted through the papers looking for any information about Hershel. I found the one about the Firebird Airlines trial.

"Huh. It looks as though he was the presiding judge for that trial."

"Interesting." Zelda made a note of that in her notepad.

"And check this out." Alex paged through some of the other documents. "The mechanic made an unsuccessful attempt to appeal after the trial."

"Yeah." Shannon read over Alex's shoulder. "Too bad the mechanic's name is blacked out."

The black ink censoring the name had been printed with the document; there was no way to figure out the hidden name.

"There must be a reason for this."

I sat back and pondered. "Well, because I had found an ominous note in Venshlin's office, he likely knew that I would go there."

"Would that mean that Venshlin is hiding something?"

"It would seem so."

Zelda looked at a margin note written by Venshlin. "It looks like Hershel knew someone at Firebird Airlines."

"What do you mean?"

Zelda read a note in the margin. "'Way to keep a secret, Marty. I'm sure your brother-in-law would be thankful for the job you swindled from that Firebird mechanic.'"

"Hmm…" Richard thought back to the murder trial. "It did seem that Venshlin was a bit hostile toward Hershel."

"But if Hershel's brother-in-law was indeed wanting to work at Firebird Airlines," Shannon wondered, "then why was Hershel chosen to preside over the Firebird lawsuit trial?"

Alex shrugged. "Maybe he was the only judge that was available."

Zelda rebutted him. "Venshlin said that no one knew of Hershel's brother-in-law."

That's when a thought occurred to me. "What are the odds of a lawyer and a judge involved in the same lawsuit trial to also be involved in the same murder trial six years later?"

"The chance is small, but their records show that they were never together between those two trials."

"So, Venshlin has killed two people involved in a class action lawsuit trial; the defense attorney and the judge. He also killed a veteran police detective."

Richard adjusted his hat. "What's your point?"

"Do you think that Venshlin could also be targeting the prosecution attorney from that trial?"

Zelda read another of Venshlin's notes. "'Nelson Kurt Yitzhak, the prosecutor, did not contribute to the verdict; it was the exclusionary rule and Satchel's ostentatious reputation that led to the outcome. What's more, the failed appeal of the ex-mechanic was down to the incompetent appeal attorney. Gary McCrery quite contrary, how your flowers will grow.'"

"Wait… Gary McCrery? Does he mean the DA?"

"Yeah. He was also the ex-mechanic's attorney at his appeal hearing. 'You ought to have retired when you found out about your brain cancer. Maybe then, the ex-mechanic could have gotten himself reinstated.'"

"Does that mean Venshlin is going to kill McCrery?"

"Only fate and time will tell."

Zelda got all of the documents in a stack and put them back in the box.

Chapter XVII

The Backstab

It felt awkward sitting on the opposite side of the desk in the interrogation room. And frankly, I knew I shouldn't have to answer the questions that would come my way.

"Tell me about what you did on the evening of March 4th, 20—." Rachel paced back and forth on her side of the desk.

"My friends and I were discussing the outcome of the trial from that day at the diner."

"What trial was this?"

"The murder trial of William York."

"Where did you go after you left the diner?"

"I went to the Landenberg Law Firm."

"Why did you go to Landenberg?"

"I was investigating my prime suspect for the murders, Zachary Venshlin."

"Do you know for a fact that he did this?"

"The evidence I have is circumstantial, but I am in my entirety persuaded that Zachary Venshlin is a saboteur and a murderer. Furthermore, I have reason to believe that he's really someone else."

"What evidence do you have to support your theory?"

"I have received a note before each murder took place, and the fire that killed my dad happened at Wainwright, which is where Venshlin went to law school at."

"So, what did you find at Landenberg?"

"I found a large number of documents about each of the flopped trials over the last five years, which Venshlin had been studying greatly."

"Do you have any of those documents from Venshlin's office in your possession?"

"Not on my person; the last people who had them were Zelda and Shannon Thomson."

"Was that all you found there?"

"I also found an odd assortment of items in Venshlin's desk drawer that I haven't quite wrapped my mind around. As I collected the evidence and put them in bags to take to show to my friends, I came across a note presaging Hershel's death."

"Do you have that note with you?"

I searched through my pockets for about ten seconds. "No, I don't. Anyway, after I left Landenberg, I headed for the subway. I saw a bunch of people walking into the station from the train tunnel."

"Is this where you found Hershel?"

"I found him after a long walk down the tunnel. He was completely decimated by the train, but Dr. Suzuki was able to identify him through DNA and fingerprints, as well as dental and X-ray records."

"So how did Hershel get there in the first place?"

"That I don't know."

It was clear that Rachel didn't believe me. "So, what do you believe is the motive for committing these crimes?"

"We're still juggling with that; all we have so far is the evidence that was recovered from Wainwright."

Rachel started flipping through her notepad. "There's a bizarre pattern between you and these murders; you were the last person to see Satchel alive, and you were the first person to find your father dead. Not only that, you thought the person who got hit by the subway train was Judge Hershel before the medical examiner identified him."

"But I had no reason to kill any of them."

"Your father's death would coincide with his skill as a detective; he had to be put down to keep him from solving the mystery of Satchel's death."

"But why would I kill Satchel or Hershel?"

"Maybe you didn't have a motive, but you certainly had the capacity to kill them. Do you want to know what I think?"

I heaved a long sigh. "What?"

"I think William York is masterminding this plot."

I stood up and threw my hands on the table. "What kind of ludicrous story is that?"

"He had orchestrated the death of Harold Satchel to get a better attorney at his trial, and then you to kill his father so that he wouldn't figure out who killed Satchel."

"I don't even know William York!"

Rachel again wasn't wavered by my story. "Of course you don't."

"Venshlin had just been hired less than 24 hours before Satchel's murder; how could William have known that having Venshlin represent him would get him acquitted?"

She ignored my question. "Satchel had been the defense attorney at the Firebird Airlines lawsuit trial in 20—, and you know how many people were devastated by the trial's verdict. William York had a motive to kill Satchel: revenge. You had the time to kill him: your meeting with him before the murder. There's no denying it, Vasquez Private Eye."

"But how did William know that my father was such a skilled detective?"

"He didn't, you did. You had to finish him off yourself before he finished you and William."

"I had never been to Wainwright until the fire."

"And how could you have known it was Hershel who was hit by the train without any identifiable body parts?"

"It was the note I found in Venshlin's office."

Her eyes narrowed. "That story is flying like a noseless plane, Vasquez Private Eye."

"So, you admit that it's at least marginally plausible?" I remembered one day during my police academy student career when Richard read me one of his college notebooks about a class presentation that explained how loss of a nose in flight could cause a plane to fly upward before falling and crashing.

"I meant that your story is poorly constructed, and you know it. Anyway, I digress."

"You can't prove me guilty since I committed no crime in my life."

"I can and I will. All I need is proof that you are the killer, and I'll get to succeed my mom as police chief after she retires, while you are left without a job."

My face unraveled into shock. "You sick witch!"

She turned to her colleague standing to her left. "Please take Mr. Vasquez back home."

I was confused. "You're not arresting me?"

"The evidence I have so far is circumstantial. But I will find what I'm looking for. You're undoubtedly responsible for these deaths, Vasquez Private Eye."

I stood up to follow the officer out the door. "I think we need to compare dictionaries over the word 'undoubtedly'."

"I need a drink." I don't usually drink alcohol, but after the interrogation, I was under enough stress that I thought I had to crash at Zelda's house and get a drink.

Richard looked in the fridge. "We have some of that Black Forest cake leftover from my birthday."

Alex laughed to himself. "Does it ever bother you that your birthday only happens once every four years?"

"I'm the oldest of us five, so it doesn't matter."

"And what's bizarre about that fact is you're dating the youngest of us five."

"We both have the same age difference from Johnson, so it doesn't matter."

"That'll do." I grabbed a slice of cake and went into the living room where Zelda was waiting.

Alex noticed my anomalous behavior. "I'd say that was not a piece of cake to go through."

"No, it wasn't."

It was at that point that a knock sounded from the front door. Shannon went over to answer it.

"Hi, Professor Vasquez."

"Hi, Shannon."

Shannon led Mom into the house and sat down with me on the couch. "Under newfound stress, are we, Johnson?"

"I am."

Mom looked at me. "Why?"

"Rachel is investigating these events so she can get me fired and succeed Bethany as police chief."

Everyone was shocked. "What?"

"And she thinks that I'm committing the murders for William York, even though I've never met him in my life."

Richard got to his feet. "This is madness!"

Mom limped over to the couch where I was. "You can't be serious!"

"I kid you not. She told me that during my interrogation earlier today."

"She actually did that? What could she be thinking?"

"I wish I knew."

"I'm going to have to have a talk with Bethany about Rachel's insular behavior."

"I think that would be a good idea; she has no idea who she's after, but I do."

Shannon leaned toward my ear. "No, you don't."

Mom made her way to the door. "Well, I should hope this crime is solved before too long; I know you can do it."

As she left, Zelda continued to ask me questions. "What did Rachel say was the motive behind the murders?"

"She says that William is acting out revenge against the Firebird Airlines verdict."

Zelda thought about this. "Hmm... maybe she actually reached a viable conclusion."

"What do you mean?"

"Maybe these murders really *are* being committed out of disdain of the Firebird Airlines trial." Zelda brought up the appropriate document. "Satchel was the defense attorney, and Hershel was the judge."

I pondered this. "Yeah, Venshlin's margin notes do ring true with vengeance."

Zelda and Shannon opened up a cooler out on the back porch and put charcoal on the grill. "What's say we talk about this over lamp chops?"

I shrugged. "I guess."

CHAPTER XVIII

The Alliance

At around 5:30 PM, a knock came at the door.

When I answered it, I saw a man with very short hair and a clean-shaven face. He was wearing a brown fedora, a dark green sweater with a white collar shirt underneath, beige denim slacks, and black shoes. I could see by the look in his dreary blue eyes that he had come a long way in a desperate search of something.

I dusted myself off and straightened my posture for the impromptu guest. "Can I help you, sir?"

"That's exactly why I came."

Richard recognized his voice. "William York?"

"I'm being antagonized by the police. You need to get them to back off of me."

Zelda was at the door. "You do realize that Johnson is a policeman, right?"

"Yeah, I know that Johnson's a policeman. But that's not the problem. Some snooty policewoman claimed that I was guilty of coercing him into killing people." William turned to me. "She said she had also questioned you and that you refused to incriminate me."

I confirmed to him. "That's right."

"I'm here to ask for your help. You're also conducting an investigation into these murders, right?"

"Yes, I am."

"I need you to find a way to prove that I had nothing to do with these acts."

This was the first time I had spoken to him, and he had gotten away with murder because of Venshlin, so I was at first hesitant about accepting the request.

Ultimately, I agreed to help him as best I could. "I'll do it, William."

He ran up to me and hugged me as hard as he possibly could. "Oh, thank you so much!"

Richard seemed distrusting of William. "Johnson, that guy tried to kill my brother; why are you helping him?"

William was about to speak, but Zelda beat him to it. "Richard, there's no need to beat up on people. He's being bullied by your ex-girlfriend, so it's only right that we help him through a rough time."

William came inside and looked to Richard. "She used to be your girlfriend?"

Richard was wary of the guest, but Zelda and I made sure that William would not be harassed further. "It's a really long story."

Shannon also seemed uneasy about William, though I wasn't sure if she was just shy about the new guest or scared of him because of his crime.

"I don't believe you've had the opportunity to meet all of us." I shut the door behind William. "You probably already know me and Richard."

"Yes, I do."

"So, this is Alex Andrews, and these two are Shannon and Zelda Thomson."

He shook hands with each of them. "Was I walking in on anything?"

Richard grunted. "There's a cookout on the back porch if you…" he cringed slightly, "…want to come and join us."

Alex escorted William to the back porch. "Yeah, I'd say you get to the grill to recover from your grilling."

William laughed and got a bottle of Kirshwasser from the cooler. As he poured himself a shot, I pulled up a seat next to him, with Richard and Zelda sitting with us, and Shannon attending the grill.

"I don't understand it." He picked up his shot glass and heaved a vehement sigh. "I walk away from the courthouse a free man, and some golf-delta witch cop accuses me of being a criminal mastermind because of it."

Shannon flipped a round of sheep legs onto a serving dish. "Yeah, the world has an absurd operation."

"What am I going to do?" William started to drink his shot as his eyes glazed.

Alex started carving the sheep legs. "You can always go to a new place to start a new life. Maybe New York?"

William shot the liquor out his nose and cracked up.

"Maybe a game of darts can help." I went over to the dartboard on the other side of the porch.

"Yeah, okay." He set the empty shot glass on the table and came over.

As we started playing the game, I decided to strike up a conversation with William.

"So, aside from being lambasted by Rachel, how have you been, William?"

William shrugged. "Well, I've been struggling to make ends meet; I haven't been able to get a job for years."

"You had been acquitted just last week."

"I meant before my father died."

"Oh, yeah. Patrick had said in court that your dad had mentioned you being unemployed for a while."

"Right. I just need a way to get some money."

"I think Alex was looking to hire someone at his store. Maybe you can ask him."

"Where's that at?"

"Dr. Chuckle's Prank Lab and Gag Shop."

He seemed to flinch at the name. "I don't know."

"What do you mean?"

"I heard that place is haunted."

"Haunted?"

"There are rumors that some sort of secret agent roams the streets at night hunting down criminals."

"What does that have to do with Alex's store?" I knew what the answer was, but my friends and I weren't about to tell.

"During my stay in jail, I've heard stories about inmates being captured by this guy and taken to the shop where the police come to pick them up."

"I see. Well, I'm not sure how much Alex knows about this, but you can ask and find out."

"From what I've been told, the police interrogated him about this guy (who goes by the name Brandon Chide), and he claims that he was serving as a night guard at the shop."

"Yeah?"

"Doesn't that seem a little bit overkill? And how does Chide know about all these crimes?"

"Beats me." I went over to retrieve the darts from the board to start another round.

As I did so, I filled him in on the clues we found. "So, anyway, we believe that whoever killed these three men is somehow involved in these court cases going wrong."

"How do you figure that?"

I reached into my pocket. "I received this note while I was talking to Satchel about a string of court cases that had acquitted truly guilty defendants."

Richard stuck his fork in his biscuit like a flagpole. "I know you were one of those defendants."

I glared at Richard. "Now's not the time, Richard."

"Well, he did!" He lunged from his seat toward me, but he was quickly restrained by Zelda and Shannon.

William and I resumed our discussion, ignoring Richard as he struggled to wrestle himself free from the tight grasp of Shannon and Zelda.

He read the note I had found in the restaurant. "Yeah, it would seem that there is a sabotage operation with all of these court cases. And the perpetrator is also responsible for killing these three men."

"Right. I have suspicions that the attorney that defended you at the trial is responsible."

"How do you figure that?"

I got out the note I discovered before I had ended up at Wainwright. "His name appeared at the bottom of this note."

"The first victim was Harold Satchel, right?"

"Yeah. He was kidnapped while he and I were en route to the police station where you were, and then stabbed in the throat with an icicle."

"How is that possible? Or more to the point, how do you know?"

"The medical examiner found evidence that Satchel had been stabbed with some kind of stake. A piece broke off in the body, but the lodged piece somehow disappeared."

"And it was from that that you discerned the weapon as being made of ice?"

"That and a facetious comment from Alex."

"Alright. Did the fire at Wainwright have anything to do with this?"

"Yeah. My dad was killed there."

"He was killed because of the fire?"

"His death was the cause of the fire."

"What do you mean?"

"He was bound in a closet and burned alive."

"Is that why you're investigating this?"

"Yeah."

"What about the third murder?"

"I had suspicions about your attorney, and so I searched through his office to find out as much about him as I could. As I was investigating the place, I found evidence of an interest with the Firebird Airlines trial of 20— and this third note. I left to tell my friends, and I stumbled upon the crime scene on the way here."

"Were you able to figure out who it was?"

"Yeah, it was Judge Hershel."

"You mean the guy who presided over my murder trial last week?"

"That's the one."

"What's going on here?"

"That's what we're trying to figure out. But we do have a good idea of why they were killed."

William read the third note I had collected. "This guy is good at writing poetry."

"Yeah. So, what happened was I was the last person who saw Satchel alive, I ended up at Wainwright during the fire that killed my father, and I came across the murder site of Hershel on my way home from Landenberg."

"And how did I end up in the mix?"

I started thinking about that. "From what I believe, it may have been because I had mentioned Satchel serving as the defense attorney in the Firebird Airlines lawsuit."

"Yeah, I remember that."

"She thinks that the murders have something to do with the outcome of that trial."

"Do you think so?"

"I'm considering that as a possible motive. If we could figure out who would have a motive, then we might be able to understand who Zachary Venshlin is."

"Wait—who he is?"

"Yeah."

"You mean he's someone else?"

"That's right. And I will find the evidence lest my name not be Johnson Charlie Clayton Vasquez."

CHAPTER XIX

Zelda's Story

Finally, my story is in here. I'm pretty sure that you've already read what my sister wrote. As you know, she doesn't like Alex due to his carefree jesting. And she had whipped up a type of sugar that led to Alex's secret life as Brandon Chide.

And all the others have given their perception about the Firebird Airlines crash and the influence it had on them. So, it would be discourteous for me not to.

On the evening of the flight, I was driving to the airport to pick up Johnson after he landed. I was listening to the radio when the news started talking about a plane crash in Kansas City, Missouri. The newsman seemed happy, but the news was anything but.

As I listened, I thought to myself, "I hope those people made it out okay."

The newsman continued. "Many of the passengers and crew did survive the crash, including one passenger who sent out a distress message."

The radio broadcasted the message. When I heard that, I slammed on the brakes and nearly got rear-ended by the car behind me; that was Johnson's voice!

As soon as I recovered from my shock, I raced homed and packed my bags to drive to Kansas City.

During the drive, Johnson called me to say that he and his family were on the flight on their way home from Denver. They all survived, (except Terrence) and they were spending the night at Kansas City hospital.

When I arrived at the scene, it was clear that something big had happened. The plane was lying parallel to the riverbank on which it rested, the roof peeled open like a candy wrapper. A thick layer of soot and ashes surrounded the fuselage.

On the plane's left side, the side facing the river, I could see the red and orange lettering with a turquoise trim spelling out "Firebird" clearly against the yellow background.

Further down the river, I could see the plane's vertical fin lying in the mud. Between it and the river, I could see a long trail of narrow channels leading to the runway nearby, which must have been from the tail hitting the beach before skidding across the river.

The NTSB's go team arrived two minutes after I did. I decided to monitor whatever I could about the investigation and look for answers to my own questions, hoping that I could understand what had caused the plane to crash.

From the way the plane hit the river, it was clear that the fin was the first thing to break off the plane. Now it was up to the NTSB to figure out how it happened.

The plane's black boxes were recovered within minutes of the team's arrival. While the recorders were taken off to be analyzed, interviews with eyewitnesses went underway.

Air traffic control told investigators about what Johnson had told them about the stabilizer failure. Sure enough, they found that the fin's leading edge was split down the middle and bent outward. The rivets holding it together were broken, and the discovery of the damage explained the plane's performance during the flight:

When the skin of the vertical stabilizer split, the plane became virtually un-flyable. The rapidly changing movements caused by this meant the stabilizer was under extreme stress. Soon, the connections failed, and the plane landed in the river.

The cockpit voice recorder revealed that the pilots were experiencing unusual in-flight shaking before the crisis, which they initially believed to be turbulence; air traffic control said there was no wind at all, and data from the flight data recorder showed that the "turbulence" was consistent with performance with the fin coming apart.

The fact that the aircraft was equipped with an aircraft surveillance recorder, which recorded video feeds from a series of cameras all over the aircraft, suggested that Firebird held low priority for aircraft maintenance.

While the plane's maintenance history was scrutinized for an explanation, metallurgists examined the torn stabilizer to figure out how the rivets broke.

The rivet holes had been altered in shape from circular to elliptical. The small folds of metal on the right side of each hole indicated that the rivets had pressed against the edges of the holes, which meant there was an abnormal distribution of load on the rivets.

The bottom hole was perfectly intact, which meant that it was not carrying an excessive load; the higher holes showed an increasing distortion in shape from circular to pill-shaped. This meant the failure started at the base, and the rest of the rivets must have popped like buttons on Superman's shirt.

So, they now had to figure out what had caused the first rivet to break to start with.

The rivets had all broken in half fairly cleanly, and the bottom half of each rivet was still embedded in the fin; five had broken due to overload, while the sixth rivet had broken due to metal fatigue. The fatigued rivet wasn't perfectly straight, and there were a number of tiny cracks on the inward side of the bend; that meant the rivet must have been straightened from a bent state.

The plane's last maintenance operation was carried out seven weeks before the crash. The workers were interviewed, and sure enough, the rivets on the vertical stabilizer's skin had been replaced. Records showed nothing unusual about the rivets, but the mechanics said the rivets were the last of that particular type in stock at the time, so there wasn't much of a concrete lead to find out if anything could have been faulty about them.

They soon found, however, that the remaining rivets were one short of what was required. The mechanic overseeing the operation said he was unable to obtain more rivets, so he improvised with an out-of-shape but correctly sized rivet which he found on the floor and hammered straight.

Seven week later, as the plane flew over Kansas City, the defective rivet failed, killing 75 people.

It seemed a bit hasty to blame one man for this crash. It prompted me to investigate further to see if the mechanic was squarely to blame, or if there was a bigger reason behind the breakdown in the shop.

I discovered a phone call from the mechanic to the CEO of Firebird Airlines, Nicholas Althorn. I called Althorn to gain some information about the exchange.

As it turned out, the mechanic had been trying to find a batch of new rivets for several days before the operation, and Althorn had refused to fulfill the requests that came to him. It baffled me that Althorn wouldn't buy any new rivets for the mechanics despite numerous requests.

When I asked Althorn about his repeated refusal with buying replacement airplane parts, his answer almost made me cut my ear off, because I couldn't believe what I heard.

"We need money to train new pilots, and so we don't have the capacity to shop for parts."

If Richard had been the one talking, he'd have slammed the receiver hard enough to break off the hook.

I talked to the pilots of Flight 934, as well as a number of other Firebird pilots, and they explained that their training involved handling a number of extreme and unusual structural and mechanical failures which hardly any other airline would have even thought to train their pilots for. It was evidence that planes falling apart were far from rare at Firebird Airlines.

I investigated further into Firebird Airlines' history and uncovered a list of incidents as long as Althorn's arm.

Four months before Flight 934, a plane suffered a loss of aileron control flying over Little Rock. Using the throttles to steer, the pilots managed to land safely with no injuries.

In November 20—, two people on the ground were hit by a piece of an engine cowling that fell off a 767 flying over Iowa. The plane spiraled down to the ground and landed safely in Chicago.

At least five planes were found to have been the victim of the landing gear collapsing on landing. Sixty-seven people in total were injured.

And that's just to name a few.

In all cases, improper maintenance and/or lack of any maintenance caused the incidents.

In the Little Rock incident, the hydraulic lines for the ailerons had been sealed with epoxy; it was shaken loose by the plane's vibrations, causing a leak.

The engine cowling separation in Iowa had occurred because the rivets holding up the bottom half were rusty when they were first installed; they were never replaced by Firebird's mechanics.

And in each of the landing gear failures, the tires had never been replaced or re-inflated since the plane had been purchased by Firebird Airlines. The loss of the tires caused the tires to burst, shearing the hub bolts and transferring abnormal forces to the landing gear pylons.

But because the pilots had been trained to handle all of those situations, no one was killed in any of them. Firebird Airlines, therefore, didn't feel subpoenaed to change any of its maintenance practices, nor did the FAA take steps to get that to happen.

Now they had 75 souls resting under the waters of the Missouri River.

I published my findings, and it made front page news. Almost immediately, a class-action lawsuit was filed against Firebird Airlines for its poor maintenance regime.

But when the case was taken to court, the airline was acquitted of all charges.

I spent the next four years looking through law books to understand how it all happened. None of the resources I looked through was enough to give me an explanation.

Chapter XX

The Involvement

It was at that time that Mom returned to the house and joined us all on the back porch. "Is everyone doing okay?"

"Yes, we're fine, Mom."

She walked over to where William was sitting. "Who are you?"

William got up. "I'm William York."

Mom shook his hand. "Martha Vasquez."

"I'm guessing you're Johnson's mother?"

"Yes, I am."

William seemed to recognize Mom. "Aren't you one of the forensics teachers at Deviltry University?"

"Yes, I am."

Shannon nodded. "I was one of her students."

Mom shut the back door behind her. "So, what's been going on around here?"

"Your son has been investigating a string of murders in the area, and the police chief's daughter is blaming me and him for these crimes."

"Yeah, he told me about that before you showed up." She limped over to an empty seat at the table.

William noticed the reason for her lopsided tottering. "So, what'd you do to your leg there?"

She looked down and sighed. "I was involved in a plane crash about seven years ago. My younger son was killed in that accident, and I haven't felt the same since."

"Oh. Well, that's rather unfortunate."

"Yeah. And what hurts worse is that the airline was left completely off the hook for its actions which caused the crash to happen."

"I don't blame you." He also seemed equally devastated about that fact. She shifted her attention to me. "So, what do you have so far?"

Zelda took a sip from her water glass. "Well, Johnson is suspicious about the attorney that had defended William at the murder trial."

"Why's that?"

William twirled his fork. "Johnson's been receiving a number of notes that have been foreshadowing the murders of three men. According to Johnson's suspicions, my attorney, Zachary Venshlin, wrote his name at the bottom of the second note, and your husband was killed in a fire at the Wainwright Law Academy, where Mr. Venshlin had studied law. On top of that, I was acquitted by Venshlin at my murder trial last week, which seems to parallel other controversial verdicts from other recent trials."

"Yeah, I've heard about that." Mom heaved a sigh. "He definitely crossed the line with sabotaging the kidnapping trial."

Richard mopped his eyes and stood up with his hands slammed on the table. "Why is everyone being nice to some dixie that got away with trying to kill my brother?"

Mom was quick to admonish him for his unruly actions. "Richard Edward Avery Ralston, that's no way to treat a man like William!"

"Well, he did!"

Mom was on her feet in a flash, and she glared into his eyes. "I don't want to hear another word from you, young man. Is that clear?"

Richard nodded in silence.

Zelda finished her meal. "So, how have you been doing lately, Professor Vasquez?"

Mom let off a whoosh of air. "I'm managing. I'm sure if my husband were still alive, he'd be able to sort through this mess in no time."

"That's what I think was Venshlin's motive for killing him; he was such a good detective, so he had to be silenced. Though Rachel had questions as to how he got close to him."

William poured himself a shot of Kirsch. "Yeah, he was definitely a legend."

Richard got up from the table. "I'm going inside; does anyone need anything?"

All of us shook our heads.

"Alright." With that, he disappeared through the door.

Mom opened the cooler and started delving through it. "So, were Satchel and my husband the only people that were supposedly killed by this Venshlin guy?"

"Uh, no." William finished his shot. "Judge Hershel is dead, too."

I nodded. "He got hit by a train in a subway tunnel after William was acquitted."

"I see." She shut the cooler and sat down with a bottle of iced tea. "Do you know if anyone else is at risk?"

"We're not entirely sure, but we suspect that there may be a fourth victim sometime in the future."

"Who do you think it could be?"

"We think that it might be an attorney involved in the ex-Firebird mechanic's appeal trial."

William went to the cooler to get himself another shot of Kirsch.

"You've already had two shots, William."

William seemed cavalier. "Do I look like I care?"

I was surprised. "Hey, I'm just trying to help the two of us through this mess."

William returned to the cooler, and then suddenly spoke up. "Where did that come from?"

I turned to him. "What?"

He took out a folded note. "I found this in the cooler on top of the Kirsch bottle."

"Let me see that." I unfolded the note as the rest of the people swarmed around me for a look.

As I predicted, there was another poem.

Maybe you're picking up the pattern here
Certainly so, being governed by fear
Crazy it seems, but

Really, it's sane
Except that its sickness is hard to feign
Ready to rest? Go ahead, have fun
Yet even now, I still am not done

21, 9, 24, 11, 12, 22, 1

That's when I was struck by a sense of panicking dread. "Oh, my prophetic soul!"

William looked at the three poems we had already and compared it to the newly acquired fourth one. "Is that saying what I think it's saying?"

I nodded. "We need to find McCrery and warn him!"

Zelda pointed out a major obstacle. "You are aware that none of us knows where he is right now. We'll have to find him before we can tell him."

Mom got out her phone to look up McCrery's address. "1527 Reendow Mill Street."

I hopped in the cruiser with Zelda, Mom, and William and raced to McCrery's place, hoping to warn McCrery before Venshlin came knocking. Richard, Shannon, and Alex took his van and followed us.

As we pulled up, I could see Rachel stepping out of a cruiser that was parked in the driveway.

Rachel and I confronted each other and we both spoke simultaneously. "What are you doing here?"

Rachel caught sight of William. "You two *are* working together. I knew it."

William stood beside me. "We are working alongside one another, but we're not partners in crime."

"Yeah, uh-huh. I'll believe you when both of you get killed by your suspect."

I repeated my question. "So, what are you doing here, Rachel?"

"A burglary had been reported here," she thumbed the white house that stood twenty feet away, "and I'm going inside to investigate."

Before anyone could speak further, she turned and went inside the house.

I sighed and looked to the nearby path.

There were footprints and drag marks leading to a barn up on the hill. We made our way up to it, and we saw the barn door was ajar.

The barn was pretty dark save for light which seeped in through the cracks in the walls. Dust hung in the air tinting the shadows amber. A tractor was situated on the other side of the barn, as well as a tool rack.

"What are we doing here?" Richard dug a pitchfork out from under a pile of hay on the floor and leaned it against a post. "Shouldn't we be searching the house to find McCrery?"

"Rachel's in the house; we can't search there."

Mom nodded. "Plus, there's a trail of drag marks going from the house to the barn, so there's likely to be something in the barn that's worth finding."

The barn door burst open.

"VASQUEZ!" Rachel marched over to me as I started to scramble up the ladder.

I started fleeing across the unstable wood floor, Rachel pursuing me while the others watched from below. Floorboards creaked and buckled under my feet as I absconded precariously through the dusty wooden barn.

As I looped around back to the ladder, I stepped on a weak floorboard and fell through, landing on a haystack.

I was quick to recover from the landing and collect my bearings.

As I looked around to confirm that I was uninjured, I made a disheartening discovery.

A body tied up with power cords smacked us with the sobering fact that we had arrived too late.

Gary Evan Thomas McCrery was dead.

CHAPTER XXI

Murder #4

It was a hypnotizing scene, yet at the same time rather lackluster. The victim was perforated with multitudinous tiny puncture wounds. It seems an impossible scenario, and yet here I was, looking at it with seven other people.

On the wall above the body, written in blood and wood burns, there was a message.

Remember what you found back at my school?
Effortless finds are a useful tool
Veneered in straws are the weapons you seek
Eighty in total
No reason to freak
Good luck with trying to find each one
Enjoying a laugh with a literal pun

Rachel looked through the hole I fell through, and she whispered to herself "What could those men be thinking?"

I got up and dusted myself off. "How long do you think it would take to do something like this?"

William picked up the piece of wood that I stepped on. "We could be here for days if we tried to count all of the stab wounds on him."

Zelda was taking pictures of McCrery's body and the poem on the wall. "We'll leave that to the medical examiner. Then we can get an estimate of how long the killer was here."

Shannon couldn't understand the scene that lay before her. "So, what happened with McCrery?"

Zelda responded. "It looks like he was stabbed to death hundreds of times with needles."

Richard looked at the poem. "So, what did they do, bury the needles in the haystacks?"

I put on my gloves. "It would seem like it. Let's go get searching through here."

"I've heard of searching for a needle in a haystack, but this is ridiculous." Alex was inevitably going to say it.

Rachel started to climb down the ladder. "I'm not going to stick around for this."

I snickered. "And yet you want to solve this case before I do? No wonder you failed with Richard."

She snapped back from the tractor. "Hey, you were the one that persuaded Rickey to stop dating me!"

"No, that was Zelda."

Rachel huffed like the Big Bad Wolf and stormed out of the barn to leave.

William chuckled. "Witches be crazy, I tell ya."

I nodded. "Ain't that the truth?"

Mom turned to follow out the door. "Well, I don't think there anything more I can do here."

I agreed. "Yeah, I don't think you should go around and look through here with that bad knee."

"It'd probably be helpful if you had magnets and metal detectors to help you look."

Everyone was assigned to a different haystack to search through. If the writing on the wall was true, there were eighty needles hidden amongst the dozens of haystacks throughout the entire barn.

"Are you sure the needles are even here at all?"

"If Venshlin is hiding them, this would be an ideal spot to hide them."

As you would expect, we were searching the barn for hours. We didn't have any metal detectors with us, which made the task even more difficult. As time dragged on from minutes to hours, the lack of food and water was beginning to take its toll on us.

Alex yawned, still dressed in his "Dr. Chuckle" attire. "I'm about ready to hit the hay."

Shannon lethargically rolled her eyes and recited a line from Romeo and Juliet, indicating that she was wanting Chide to come out soon.

Pretty soon, all six of us had fallen asleep in whatever haystack we were looking through.

I woke up to find myself looking up at a "no smoking" light. I was confused, so I looked to my left to find out where I was. I could see clouds below me, most of which were being obscured by an airplane wing and engine.

"Wait—why am I on a plane?"

I turned to my right, and I saw that Harold Satchel was sitting next to me. "Wh-what are you—how did you get here?"

Gary McCrery was sitting across the seat aisle from me. "Ees et not obfious?"

I was confused. As I opened my mouth to speak, Judge Hershel came up and sat down next to McCrery. "Did I miss anything?"

McCrery got up to let the judge back in his seat by the window. "Vell, Chonson had voken up a vew zeconz ago, but osser zan zat, nussing."

Then, Dad wheeled a drink cart up to us. "Would you gentlemen like something to drink?"

Satchel and McCrery both requested Coke and ginger ale respectively, while Hershel asked for apple juice.

Dad then turned to me. "And how about you, son?"

I couldn't understand what I was seeing. All four of the men I was seeing were dead. And why was I on an airplane?

"I'll just have water." Despite being starving to death moments ago, I didn't feel hungry for some reason.

Dad gave my water to Satchel, who then passed it to me. I didn't want to sound rude in pointing out that everyone I was seeing was supposed to be dead, but I felt I would have to tell them at some point.

As Dad wheeled the cart forward, the two lawyers and the judge turned to me.

Satchel opened his can of Coke and put it on the tray. "You don't look very good, Johnson."

"Am I dreaming?"

"Jes, jou are." McCrery opened his can of ginger ale. "Jou are asleep een my barn vere I vas keeled."

"So, you all know you're dead?"

"Yes." Hershel took a sip of his juice.

"So, if I'm dreaming, is it still reasonable to ask why I'm on a plane with four murdered men?"

"Yes, it is." Satchel took a drink from his can. "We're trying to get a message across to you."

"And what's that?"

McCrery took a sip of his drink. "Ve can't tell jou een a sdaitforvard manner; jou haff to feegure out jourself."

"What do you mean?"

"Do you think that someone who is dead could give you answers in real life when you're awake?" Hershel finished his juice box.

"Gee, that helps a lot. Zelda is the one with that kind of sagacity, not me."

"Perhaps you should tell her about this, then." Satchel finished his drink.

"Who would believe something like this? I'm not sure *I* believe what I'm seeing."

That's when a vaguely familiar feminine voice came on the intercom. "Good afternoon, ladies and gentlemen, this is your captain speaking. We will be expecting a slight delay on our arrival to Denver. We should be expecting to land in about two hours."

I stopped my urge to identify the voice, instead sighing resignedly as the intercom clicked off. "I'm going to go crazy when I wake up, aren't I?"

Satchel and Hershel shrugged casually.

McCrery was the only one who answered. "Zat jou vill haff to anzer jourself."

Dad came back to collect the trash. He noticed I never touched my water. "Something wrong, son?"

Satchel turned to him. "He's fine, Daniel. He just needs some space, that's all."

"Very well, then."

Hershel gave Dad the empty juice box. Satchel finished off his drink, removed the tab, and gave the can to Dad.

"I'm shust takeeng my time vis mine."

Dad went to the galley behind us.

Looking around, I saw that the three people sitting with me were the only passengers on board; all the other seats in the plane were empty.

As I turned to look out the window, the plane began to shake. I grabbed my armrests, but the three people sitting with me didn't react. The shaking kept getting worse, and I began to freak out.

On the ground below, I could see a wide river carving through the grassy plains. From the way the plane was flying, I thought we were nose-diving straight in the river.

I woke up with a start. William was holding me, and I saw Richard, Shannon, and Zelda looking at me. I could tell they all slept soundly.

"Did you have a good sleep, Johnson?" Zelda helped me up to my feet and gave me my hat.

I dusted myself off and I straightened my tie without saying a word. Alex emerged from a tractor cab slipping on his sneakers and glasses.

Shannon walked me over to the police cruiser outside the barn in the morning sun. "You look like you just saw a ghost or something."

I nodded. "Four, as a matter of fact."

Richard was surprised by my response. "Really? Tell us about it, then."

I told them about the "flight" I had taken with the four murder victims.

I could tell Alex had a grand escapade last night. "Well, needleless to say, none of us found anything."

"Yeah. So, where are we going to eat?"

Chapter XXII

Numb Fingers

Later that afternoon, we returned to the barn to continue the search for the needles. This time, we had metal detectors to help us. It would have been great help earlier, though.

"Tell me again why we're doing this." Shannon was all but hopeless about finding the needles in the haystacks.

"We're looking for physical evidence that will link the perpetrator to these crimes." Zelda was taking bloody splinters from the writing on the wall for DNA testing.

"Or at least prove me and/or Johnson innocent of these crimes." William climbed to the top floor to search there.

"Hopefully, we won't hit the hay again." Alex started waving the metal detector over another haystack.

Richard, Shannon, and I were busy on each of our own haystacks with metal detectors.

Despite the tools we had at our disposal, we were still making gallingly slow progress. None of us were sure if if we did find a needle that it would be the last one to be found.

I heard a chirp from my detector, which sounded rather shrill for finding a needle; there may have been a bigger piece of metal in the haystack.

I dug through the haystack, and to my surprise, I found a glass marmalade jar partly filled with blood. Everyone was stunned by the find.

"Is this what I think it is?"

"We'll have Shannon confirm that."

"She can do it tonight if she wants."

"Yeah, I can do that."

"Let's keep looking for the needles."

It was about three weeks before we found them all. And true to the poem, there were eighty needles in total.

By the time we got to his office, Dr. Suzuki had written up his autopsy report.

"Hey, how's it going, Dr. Suzuki?" I was anxious to see if we could finally get some proof to finally vindicate me and William, and/or find the real culprit.

"These are getting more and more unusual with each of these victims." He mopped his forehead with his hand as he sighed heavily.

"So, what do we have here?"

"The victim had been stabbed thousands of times with needles or pins or something of the like."

"Yeah, we had established that fact after we had arrived at the crime scene. The weapons were there, but they had been buried in haystacks in the barn. Fortunately, we were able to find them all."

"Well, the body has been reclaimed by McCrery's son, so we cannot physically compare the weapons to the injuries."

"At least there's still some dried blood on the needles." Shannon was busy analyzing said needles. While we waited for the results, Zelda and I continued to discuss the evidence we had with Dr. Suzuki.

"So, what have you found out so far?"

"From what I can tell, he was alive during every one of the needle insertions. Assuming that the killer stopped inserting needles when the victim was dead, the whole thing must have happened in about an hour."

"During the search, we found a jar of blood in one of the haystacks. The blood was a match for Satchel's DNA."

"Do you have the jar with you?"

"Yes, I do." I gave it to Dr. Suzuki.

He reviewed the arc-shaped puddle outside the puncture wound on Satchel's neck and compared it to the jar of blood I found in McCrery's barn.

It was a perfect match.

"So, now we know why there was so little blood at the scene of Satchel's murder."

Zelda nodded. "Above the spot where we had found McCrery dead, there was a poem written on the wall in blood. The blood was tested, and it matched McCrery and Satchel; a third person was identified, but we don't know who it is other than it isn't William York."

I rubbed my chin. "Hmm… this scheme seems to have been planned for months."

"Or even years."

"It couldn't have been too long if the whole thing arose from the Firebird 934 controversy."

Shannon came back with the test results of the blood on the needles. "It's conclusive; all the blood on the needles came from Gary McCrery."

Dr. Suzuki turned to Shannon. "May I take a look at the needles? I need to confirm that these are in fact the tools used in the murder."

Shannon gave the bags with the needles to Dr. Suzuki, who proceeded to review the autopsy report on McCrery.

"How many holes were there?"

"There were 1,760 stab wounds."

Zelda let off a long whistle of amazement. "Well, let us know when you have all the measurements and an answer as to whether they were used to commit the murder."

In the meantime, I called up William York.

"Hey, Johnson." I could tell that William was drunk.

"Hey, William. We managed to find all of the needles in the haystacks, and we have proof that you had nothing to do with the crimes."

"And what's that?"

"The blood on the wall matched Satchel and McCrery, and there was a third identification that didn't match you, me, or any of my friends."

"Alright. So, what's the plan after your meeting with the medical examiner?"

"I'm thinking I come pick you up, get you up to speed on the findings, and then tell Rachel about our conclusions."

"Sounds like a plan."

"Good. And until I get there, don't go out driving."

"Right." There was a brief moment of drunken laughter before William hung up.

It was about half an hour later that Dr. Suzuki finished his assessment. "It's conclusive."

"Yeah?"

"All 80 of those needles that you found were used in the murder of Gary McCrery."

"Okay, it looks like we have everything we need."

"Shall we go and pick up William?"

"Yes, let's do that."

William had sobered up by the time we got to his house that afternoon. Either that or he was never actually drunk when I called him. But knowing whether or not he was drunk was not a priority of mine.

All I cared about was proving to Rachel that we had the right suspect and that neither of us was responsible for any of the deaths that had happened.

In the house, I took a look in the kitchen where William was cleaning a coffee pot. There was no evidence of the scene that Patrick had witnessed; a new microwave was installed, the surrounding walls were intact, and it appeared that each of the cupboards had a fresh coat of wood stain.

"You ready to head out, William?"

"Is Richard coming with us?"

"All five of us will be going, but we'll do whatever is necessary to make sure Richard behaves himself."

"Alright, then. Let's go."

Rachel was at her apartment, and my friends and I went over there to show Rachel the results from the tests. William was eager to prove his innocence.

Rachel was obviously nonchalant in what we had to tell her. "Come to turn yourself in, William?"

I stepped between Rachel and William. "I've found the needles that were used to kill McCrery."

"Oh, really?"

"Take a gander for yourself." I showed her pictures of the needles recovered from the haystacks. "These are needles from the stitching store on Bruit Road."

"He still could've bought them."

"But here's something else we found." I showed her the DNA test report. "The blood on the needles we found was from McCrery. The poem written on the barn wall was in the blood of Satchel, McCrery, and a third person whom we know wasn't William. We suspect that the third person may be the killer."

"So, who is the killer, then?"

"We haven't figured that out yet. But we do have proof that William did not kill any of the four men."

"Well, unless you can find the person who did do it, I have no choice but to hold firm in saying that you two are the ones responsible for these murders."

I was bewildered. We've proven that William was not guilty of the murders, but Rachel wouldn't listen. She started to close the door...

POW!

William punched Rachel right in the eye and took off down the hall.

Rachel was thrown back by the punch, but she quickly managed to pick herself back up. Not only did she have a black eye, there were pieces of glass in her eye, which was bleeding profusely.

Grabbing the undamaged half of her glasses from the floor, she immediately shouted, "Get the foxtrot back here, you son of a beast!"

She took off after William, who was streaking down the stairs. My friends and I followed her, worried that she would do something bad with William.

Thirty seconds later, we heard noises outside; the sound of tires screeching, followed by a loud thud, and then people started screaming.

Outside the apartment complex, there was a bus with a bloody dent on the front. On the curb in front of the bus lying in a mangled position was William York.

CHAPTER XXIII

The Loss

The passengers from the bus came out to see what had just happened. One passenger knelt beside the mangled, bloody body that the bus had struck just 15 seconds earlier.

"Yeah, serves you right!" Rachel yelled to the injured man lying in the road.

The passenger who was bent down beside William took his pulse. "He's still alive. He'll be okay."

While Shannon called an ambulance, I led Rachel over to a private area to confront her about her recklessness.

"What's with you blaming me and William for all these deaths? You're ignoring a lot of crucial evidence, being insular with your analyses, and misleading the people who are working with you on these events."

"You're at each crime scene before a murder is found, you have the capacity to carry out each murder, and William had a motive for each victim. By deduction, you and he are both in this together."

"I've collected an ample supply of evidence that will vindicate him and me."

"But, you're not an official investigator in this case, and so your evidence cannot be used. Therefore, your argument is invalid. And besides, Vasquez Private Eye, my mother was the one who approved of me leading this investigation."

"Only because you're her daughter, and you begged her to put you there."

"Either way, she says that you're more involved in this business than you think, so you should stay out of this."

"Yeah, I know that I'm involved in this personally; my father was killed by this maniac. That's why I'm investigating this mayhem in the first place."

"I can get you fired if I want to."

"You're never going to find him."

"Why would I? You and William are behind all of this anyway, so why should I bother?"

"So why have you not arrested either me or William if you think we're responsible for this carnage?"

"As I've said before, all of the evidence I have so far is circumstantial."

"That's because all you've been doing here is jumping to conclusions and basing your entire investigation off of those assumptions. I know for a fact that you're just in this for the attention. I have no intentions of becoming a police chief, and I could solve this easier than you can."

"What, you think a dim-witted, lazy-eyed, uncommitted rookie cop could end a spree of shoddy court cases?"

"I'm only a rookie because you stole my promotion. I may be 'lazy-eyed' as you would say, but I have tools at my disposal to help me with any investigation. You just make up stories that serve your own ends. And if my father were alive, he'd show you what's what."

Rachel grabbed my tie and pulled me in her face. "Now you listen here, Vasquez. I will get my promotion to police chief, and no one is going to stand in my way."

I was thrown into a stack of trash cans.

"If you know what's good for you, you'll turn in your badge and your weapon; I don't want to see you anywhere near this investigation."

As she walked away, I muttered under my breath. "If that's how you're gonna play, that's totally fine by me."

I got back up and regrouped with the other four in time to see William being loaded into an ambulance.

Richard and Shannon climbed into the back seat of Alex's van, while Zelda and I got in the squad car. And pretty soon, we were on our way.

When we arrived, William was in the X-ray room. We waited outside until they were finished taking X-rays so that we could talk to him.

Ten minutes after we arrived, another doctor arrived to assess the X-rays taken.

"Looks like we have a broken leg, twelve fractured ribs, both humeri are broken, there are a few cracks in the skull, and the jaw seems dislocated."

"Is he going to be okay?"

"If he receives medical attention swiftly, he might be able to make a full recovery. But we need to get him in casts as soon as possible."

A bed was wheeled out of the room and down the hall. Each of us five followed, and we waited again outside the cast station while the doctors worked on William.

While we waited, Zelda and I both started looking at the X-rays taken of William.

"Those truly are significant injuries."

"Yeah, I know."

It was about an hour before William was treated and all of the doctors had gone.

Alex, Richard, Shannon, Zelda, and I entered the room. I got a chair besides William's bed and sat down. "So, how are you feeling, William?"

"Just cut off the blood supply."

"Why would I do that?" Shannon, frail and vulnerable as she was, would not have done what William did.

"I want to die."

"Hey, there's no reason to hate yourself, William. I'm here for you. Just because there's some brash and impulsive policewoman accusing you of doing something you didn't do doesn't mean you should just throw your life away."

"It's not just that, Johnson."

"What do you mean?"

William looked at Richard. "Do you know why I killed my father and tried to kill Patrick?"

"So, you could collect his insurance before the policy could be changed." Alex knew it was obvious.

"That's right. I would have been happy whether or not I did get the insurance."

"Yeah? How so?"

"Well, if I did get the insurance, I would be able to at least partly rebuild my life. If not, I would have received a life sentence or the death penalty, both of them suitable options. None of those outcomes happened."

Richard folded his arms. "Well then, why did you plead 'not guilty' and insist that your father accidentally set himself up for his own death if you really did kill him and you wanted the death penalty?"

"My lawyer told me to do it."

"Why?"

"He said that I still had a chance to reclaim what I had lost in my life."

"I understand that you had been out of work when your father was killed."

"Yeah. And I was fired for no foxtrotting reason except for the company to save their own golf-delta alphas!"

"What happened?"

He took a few breaths to calm himself down.

"Seven years ago, I worked as an airplane mechanic for Firebird Airlines. A plane crash took place in Kansas City, and I was blamed for supervising a shoddy maintenance operation on the plane seven weeks before the incident."

I was intrigued at the mention of Firebird Airlines and a seven-year-old plane crash, but I didn't say anything about it.

"Evidently, the rivets holding the front of the vertical stabilizer together had been damaged during the operation. One of them had been badly bent out of shape. It was the right size for the stabilizer, and there weren't enough rivets to complete the job. The airline wouldn't give us any more, so I used a hammer to straighten out the bent rivet."

Again, the detail of him straightening the rivet grabbed my attention.

"That rivet I put at the bottom hole in the row of rivets. Seven weeks later, as the plane was flying towards Missouri, the damaged rivet succumbed to metal fatigue and snapped, and the stabilizer split in half like a hotdog bun."

"So, if it was the airline who wouldn't give you a new set of rivets, why were you shouldered with all the blame?"

"Apparently, one of the passengers sent a message to air traffic control. Someone, a friend or family member of one of the passengers or someone, heard about that message and discovered a long catalog of poor maintenance with Firebird. But they didn't know that the evidence was obtained as part of a criminal investigation into the crash without a warrant, and so all the evidence against Firebird Airlines was eliminated from being usable at the trial."

Zelda looked to me, and we could read the look in each other's eyes.

"I appealed to the NTSB to get my license back, but I ended up with Gary McCrery representing me. I thought he would be able to show that I had been scapegoated. But he couldn't, and so they still assumed I was to blame."

That finally prompted me to decide to test my hunch. "About that flight, um, that wouldn't have happened to have been Firebird Airlines Flight 934, was it?"

"Yeah, it was. I want to know who it was that gave the story to air traffic control, led Firebird Airlines' poor practices out of the courtroom, and ruined my life forever!" He clenched his hand, trying unsuccessfully to make a fist. "And when I find him, he's in for a heavy hitting."

I looked back at my friends, knowing exactly who it was he was talking about. Sure, William was in a bad state, but he could very well make good on his threat once he recovered.

I started to head out of the room, picking up speed after rounding the corner. The other four followed.

CHAPTER XXIV

The Discovery

Alex was the first to speak. "So, it was William who had supervised the bad maintenance operation on Firebird Airlines Flight 934?"

"Seems like it." Richard was surprised by the discovery that we had made.

"It all makes sense!" Zelda tied the strings together. "If William York was the mechanic, then that would explain Judge Hershel's attitude toward him."

Shannon turned to me. "So why did you run out of the room, Johnson?"

"Did you hear the last thing William said?"

"Yeah, someone on Flight 934 told air traffic control what had happened on the plane, and William ended up losing his mechanic's license as a result."

"Do you know who it was?" I kept running straight and wasn't focusing on where I was going. I reached the staircase and fell down a flight.

I hit my back on a pipe that was running up the wall, which knocked the wind out of me. I lay next to the partially open door at the bottom of the stairs gasping and moaning.

I could see my friends rushing down the stairs to where I was lying to help me.

Alex held out his hand. "Are you alright, Johnson?"

I grabbed Alex's hand and he pulled me up. "Yeah, I'm fine, thanks."

I dusted myself off and checked all my limbs and stuff to make sure I was in one piece.

That's when I noticed Mom on the stairs making her way towards us.

"Mom? What are you doing here?"

"I heard about what happened to William."

"Oh, you were going to check on him?"

"Yeah."

"Well, he's still alive, so…"

"Well, that's good."

That's when I saw a note folded under Mom's belt.

We all knew what would happen, and I picked it up to examine it.

"What's that?" Mom asked.

"Another note, I'm sure."

I unfolded it, and sure enough, another poem.

Very impressive, I must confess
Even now, there's one thing more to address
Now that you have all the clues you need,
Solve this puzzle. Very easy, indeed
Have you all the numbers from each note?
Look at them closely and see what you wrote
I have my last victim ready to kill
Now who is it? They're going to need skill

_ _ _ _ _ _ _ _ _ _ _ _ _ _ _

_ _ _ _ _ _ _ _ _ _ _ _ _ _

I turned to Alex. "Do you have the other notes that were collected?"

He reached into his pocket and took them out. "Here you go, Johnson."

"Thank you." I wrote out each set of numbers from the notes in my notepad.

8, 16, 4, 19, 14, 18, 23

3, 25, 2, 6, 17, 27, 13

10, 26, 5, 7, 15, 20, 28

21, 9, 24, 11, 12, 22, 1

Immediately, I could see the spine of the note spelled out VENSHLIN.

He *had* to be the person responsible for this mess. I was aware that Venshlin was just a pseudonym, and that he must have some sort of grudge against the justice system. More and more, it seemed to be going back to the outcome of the Firebird 934 lawsuit hearings.

Then I realized something. The numbers on each poem were all of the numbers 1 – 28 in a shuffled order. Maybe I was supposed to unscramble something to get the name of the last intended victim. But what?

Richard scratched his head. "How does Venshlin get his notes to us without anyone noticing?"

Alex shrugged. "He's a real *whiz*, I tell ya."

Mom snickered. "Maybe we can talk about this over dinner at my apartment?"

We all murmured in agreement.

We all took off our coats and shoes at the front door and sat down at the almost completely set dining room table.

Mom brought out a meal of salmon and biscuits.

As we served ourselves, Mom laid out silverware and cups for all of us. "So, have you figured out who's doing all of these crimes yet?"

"We've established a motive for the four murders. It was all part of Venshlin's revenge against the court system for acquitting Firebird Airlines. And William tried to kill himself today by running in front of a bus."

"Why did he do that?"

"It turns out he really did plan to kill his father and my brother; he was the mechanic who serviced Firebird 934 before it crashed. We've been able to discern that Zachary Venshlin is a pseudonym of someone who has blackmailed Shannon."

Mom sat down at her spot. "Blackmailed? For what?"

"I had been blackmailed into supplying someone with a potion that I invented years ago; it allows the user to assume the form of their deepest desire. Whoever it is is likely using it to become Zachary Venshlin."

"And when the five of us got drugged at Alex's store, the women became more masculine. So that would broaden the criteria of who he could be."

"But we still don't know who he really is; he could very well be anyone."

Mom returned the pot to the coaster. "Even someone in this very room?"

Richard scoffed. "That's some clichéd murder mystery horror right there."

Alex shrugged. "Ya never know."

I withdrew my fork from my mouth. "I have had just about enough accusations from Rachel, thank you very much."

Alex held his hands up. "Hey, I'm not pointing fingers at anyone."

"Venshlin's real person knew about my potion, so they must be someone who knows who I am. And all of us were at the murder trial with him."

"William didn't know any of us until after his murder trial, so he couldn't have done it. And from the fact that I have always turned into Brandon Chide at night, Johnson can't be Venshlin because he had become a drill sergeant. Patrick and William can't be him since both were with Venshlin at the trial. And he can't be Rachel, since she thought the Firebird Airlines crash was a publicity stunt."

I laid out all the notes we found and got up from the table. "How about you guys try to work out this puzzle? I'll get drinks for everyone."

"Alright."

I went into the kitchen, and the first thing I noticed was that there was a small vat of liquid on the counter. I thought it was soapy water, so I dumped it down the sink.

When I opened the glass cupboard, an empty bottle fell out. I looked at it and saw it was a bottle of sleeping pills.

I also found a huge stock of sewing needle cases in the cupboard, all of which were empty.

I laid out everything in a stack and wondered if there was anything else to find. There was nothing to find in the silverware drawer, and the oven drawer was a dead end as well.

But in the cabinet under the sink, I found a pack of cigarettes, a lighter, a bloody razor blade, several 20- and 50-dollar bills, a Kirsch bottle, and a very elaborate makeup kit which consisted of facial powder, lipstick in various colors, eye liner, hairbands, and nail polish.

This was extremely unusual.

I shut the cabinet and put all the things I found back where they originally were.

As I stood up, I noticed a large quantity of what looked like sugar scattered on the countertop near the coffee machine. I swept it into one hand to throw it out, and as it piled up in my hand, I noticed that the sugar wasn't white; it was some sort of neon greenish-orange color.

It was at that point that I realized that the coarse powder was remnants of Shannon's drink mixes.

I soon realized exactly who it was that I was up against. All the pieces fell into place as I recounted all of the clues I had. Only one piece remained.

From the dining room, I heard Zelda scream "Oh, God, no! This can't be!"

Two seconds later, Shannon shrieked. This was quickly followed by the sound of footsteps leaving the room as if the place was on fire.

When I returned, everyone was gone. The only thing I saw on the table was the note, as well as Venshlin's full name written out on a separate sheet of paper. All of the 28 letters in the name were numbered.

I noticed that many of the blanks at the bottom of the card had been filled, but not all of them. I realized what was turning up in the blanks had scared all of my friends enough to make them run off in fear without telling me anything.

I looked at the numbers from the other notes. When I compared it to the last note, I was able to fill in the rest of the blanks with the appropriate letters. When the blanks were all filled, the sharp realization hit me like a dart.

That's when my blood ran cold.

Followed by my skin crawling.

Then my fingers froze in position.

The room started to spin as I trembled.

Within seconds, I had blacked out and then collapsed unconscious on the floor.

Chapter XXV

The Revelation

When I regained consciousness, I was in total darkness. At first, I thought it was nighttime. But I soon realized I wasn't at the apartment anymore.

I had woken up sitting in a felted seat with my arms tied behind my back.

I was quickly able to make out the sound of wheels clattering on rails. Every three seconds or so, a flash of light flew past, appearing and then disappearing into the darkness.

My wrists were tied behind my back with wires, as were my feet and knees. Strangely, I wasn't gagged or tied down to where I was seated. But I knew I was in trouble.

Then the lights in the train faded on. In the dim light, I could see a large knife held close to my throat. I didn't panic or move; I simply glared at the woman holding the knife.

Her posture was skewwhiff due to her feeble knee. Her hair was dyed white, and she wore a flight attendant's uniform. She had on black lipstick, her nails were black, her skin was heavily powdered, and she had thick eyelashes.

She just stood there, dagger in hand, staring at me like I had killed the president.

I was unfazed by her demeanor as I spoke to her. "I knew it was you."

She withdrew the knife from my neck, inserted it in a holster on her thigh, and seated herself across the coach from me. "So you did. I figured you'd catch up to me soon enough."

"I know what you're planning to do."

"Oh, I can wait on that. I want to see just how good of a detective you have become." She took out a cigarette from her pocket and offered me one, which I refused.

"So, you want me to prove how I know it was you and why you did it?"

"That's right." She fished out a lighter and lit up.

"Alright, I can play by that. Let's start at the beginning, shall we?"

She blew a thin plume of smoke in my direction. "It's your report; you start wherever you please."

"You weren't aiming to destroy the justice system. You were mad at Firebird Airlines because they got away with an indescribable act. They were the reason Flight 934 crashed, but it was William York who took the blame. You impugned the justice system for mishandling the case and vowed revenge."

"So, you have the baseline down; good for you."

"You aimed your attack at the men who took part in the trial. You would rig court cases that they were involved in to acquit truly guilty defendants. But your real revenge did not lie within the courts; however, you still had business with them."

She just smirked at me; I was on the right track.

"Harold Satchel defended Firebird Airlines. He was the most skilled lawyer anyone saw. He was popular with everyone who knew him, except those who were against him in court. His skillful defense actions made him a target with you."

As I spoke, I started feeling the wires on my wrists for a knot that I could untie.

"Martin Hershel was the judge presiding over the trial. Nobody knew that his brother-in-law worked for Firebird, and he wanted to replace William York as head mechanic."

I moved the wires around my wrists to move the knot within reach of my fingers.

"When William appealed to the NTSB to reinstate his mechanic's license, his attorney was Gary McCrery. He was very poor with handling trials, and he was unable to save his client from deterioration.

"You, like thousands of others, were infuriated that the airline was let off without charge, even with the magnitude of vociferous evidence against them. So, you swore revenge. You would spend what time remained of the seven years following the crash of Flight 934 wreaking havoc on the people who served in the courtroom."

I finally located the knot and tried to untie it, which was easier said than done.

"Some time after the trial, Shannon Thomson created a drink mix which led to the creation of Brandon Chide. You managed to get a hold of the recipe, and with it, brought about your own secret identity: Zachary Venshlin. Under this alias, you enrolled into Wainwright Law Academy to learn about the justice system."

She looked up from the watch under her sleeve. "Keep going, I'm listening."

"As your education increased, you started carrying out small acts against the courts. During your four years at the law school, people were starting to get away with crimes simply because of three key people failing to correct the wrongs of a notorious airline.

"As the records piled up, you were slowly assembling your ultimatum together: killing off the men who you believe let the cause of 75 deaths go scot-free."

The knot proved difficult to work with, mostly because my hands were behind my back.

"Your first aim was the widely admired Harold Satchel. You knew Zelda and I were investigating your mayhem, and that Satchel would have pervasive knowledge of the mistrials that he represented in, so we would ask him for clues. As Satchel and I were en route to the police station to accompany William York in his interrogation, you spied on us. At the restaurant, you slipped the first of five notes into my burger wrapper after I tried to throw it away. The large crowd enabled you to be in and out without raising suspicion.

"You had an icicle which you would use to stab Satchel in the neck. You would then throw away the icicle to destroy the physical evidence. You were waiting for us on the train. With the bevy of people heading out to lunch, you could carry out your crime surreptitiously. You then collected the blood to dispose of evidence, as well as to use it later."

I finally managed to loosen part of the knot, but not so much as to pull myself free.

"There was one major obstacle to your plan: my father. You knew he would be on your trail the minute that Satchel was found under the escalator. And so, he had to be disposed of before he could expose you.

. "You had Dad kidnapped, bound him with wires, and took him to Wainwright Law Academy. You stuffed his clothes with the pages of an airplane training manual and set him on fire with a candle. You dropped your second note as I was returning to the subway station where you killed Satchel.

"The cover of the manual you left unburned as evidence of a connection to Flight 934. The manner of my father's death itself alluded to the incident as well.

"With the biggest threat eliminated, Rachel and I were soon competing to solve the mystery, the former being greedy for a promotion to police chief, I myself being hungry for revenge on my father's death. She was willing to blame me and William as the masterminds of your plot in order to get rid of my hindrance to her 'official' investigation."

She tapped a couple ashes from her cigarette onto an ashtray on the armrest beside her.

"You weren't foolish; you knew that acting too quickly following the first two murders would butter your tightrope prematurely. So, you waited until after William's murder trial had taken place. With Satchel gone, you filled in as William's new attorney. As I later found out, he had wanted to receive the death penalty at the trial. He thought you would do poorly because you were new, but he was found not guilty and let off without charge.

"I went to your office to look for clues that linked you to the murders. I found evidence that indicated that 'Zachary Venshlin' was a pseudonym, and that you had a keen interest with the Firebird Airlines trial. And that's where I found your third note.

"Of course, I had begun to catch on, but you already killed Hershel. You threw him onto the subway track, accessed by an escape passage usable only for rail employees, the means of which you acquired through your saboteur operation, and he was electrocuted by the track's third rail. He was hit by a train afterward, so his death looked like an accident.

"So once again, you waited. During that time, you were able to stock up on needles for the fourth murder.

"William was desperate to prove his innocence of your crimes, but Rachel sought to convince herself that I was under William's influence.

"Finally, it was the exit cue for Gary McCrery. After you took him to his barn and stabbed him thousands of times with needles, you hid the needles in haystacks throughout the barn, which I had to find to get any evidence against you."

She snickered to herself for a brief moment before she continued listening. I finally freed myself and placed the piece of wire on the seat beside me.

"Because I had caught on at that point, your fourth note came to my possession much later. The message on the wall was written with the blood of Satchel and McCrery.

"But even when we found the needles in the haystacks, Rachel still refused to accept the fact that William and I had nothing to do with this. Well, technically, William *had* had one thing to do with it, though nobody realized it yet. Anyway, William finally buckled and tried to kill himself. He survived to tell us that he was the head mechanic who serviced Flight 934 before it crashed. That was what got him into the mess of killing his father and trying to kill Patrick."

It was at that point that I untied the cords on my legs. I put that cord with the other one.

"Rachel believed that William had had me under his influence sabotaging the justice system as revenge for failing to serve Firebird Airlines. She knew why the operation was being committed, but she had the wrong suspect. I knew she would never solve the case as long as she pursued me and William as the culprits.

"I soon found that William was after the same person you were. I knew that the perpetrator could not be William or me. With the evidence I found after that, I knew that there was only one person with a motive and capacity to carry out these crimes. They also knew who it was that catalyzed the ultimate trashing of the Firebird Airlines trial, and I would find them even if it killed me."

She laughed at the irony of my statement, but quickly got over herself.

"With your last note, you revealed your real target. You had created the identity of your alter ego as an anagram of the victim's name, who you thought lay at fault behind the court system's failing to find Firebird Airlines' responsibility for the crash of Flight 934.

"That man was the one passenger onboard who rescued the flight crew as the plane caught fire. The passengers who survived managed to recover because he called for help on the radio. That was the first domino that ultimately led to William York being fired with Firebird evading justice. That passenger was at the heart of your revenge."

I paused a moment as my story sunk in. She took one last drag from her cigarette before I wrapped up.

"That passenger... was your only surviving son."

CHAPTER XXVI

The Confrontation

Mom and I both stood up and walked up to each other. She simply smiled as I gave her the wires I had untied from myself during my report.

Her voice took on a more seductive tone. "I must say, you've proven yourself quite well, Vasquez Private Eye." She flicked her cigarette across the coach. "Did you ever stop to think about how many people would envy the life you have?"

The cigarette ignited the carpet on the other end of the coach. But we both ignored it for now.

"What do you mean?"

"It's not every day that someone falls victim to a plane crash and lives to tell the tale. And even fewer are able to carry out an act of heroism on such an occasion."

"Understandable."

"If you hadn't stepped into the cockpit, the pilots would never have escaped. The rescue was something that many wish to achieve in their lifetime."

"I'm sure they would."

Mom moved my chin to lock my eyes with hers. "They wouldn't have known just what kind of implications would've arisen from that. It was the distress call that prompted Zelda to investigate and discover the maintenance practices of Firebird Airlines. But through the exclusionary rule, Firebird was all but out of law's reach."

Smoke wrapped around her waist from behind like they were Dad's arms. "If everyone knew that it was you who sent that message, they would have you burning away in hell like a maggot-infested pig."

She drew out her knife and once again held it up to my throat. "We can do this the easy way or the hard way. What's it going to be?"

I was pinned against the wall. One false move and I was dead. By now, the fire had taken hold, and was beginning to burn through the front of the train. The movement of the train caused the flames to lick toward us and the rest of the train, which was being shrouded with smoke. Soon, the only light in the coach was from the fire.

I made no move to push her away. "I'm guessing the easy way would be you killing me right here right now, and the hard way is waiting for the fire to consume the train."

She nodded devilishly, still holding the weapon under my chin and wearing the sadistic smirk.

I had to think fast, something I wasn't good at doing. The windows were Plexiglas, so it would be nearly impossible to break them or dislodge them. And the doors seemed unable to be opened manually, especially while the train was moving.

But despite the virulence of the situation, I knew that if I were to have any chance of getting off the train and out of harm's way, I had only one option.

I took a deep breath. "I'll choose the hard way."

Mom removed the weapon from my neck and placed it in her holster. "If that's how you want to do it. It doesn't have to be fast. I think this would be an excellent opportunity to think back on the error of your ways. And be advised that you can kill yourself at any time you please."

I didn't know if either of us would be able to escape the fire. As far as I knew, the train was driving itself, and there was no way of knowing where the train was at or was going. And only Mom knew where the train would stop, if it did. I had no idea what would come of the situation I was in. The emergency brake was out of reach, so there was almost no hope of the train being stopped by me.

Our carriage of the train was now totally ablaze, and suddenly the train ground to a halt. Mom and I both grabbed poles to avoid falling into the raging flames. The smoke that surrounding the train briefly dissipated and I could see that by sheer chance we were stopped at a station.

I sprinted through a fiery hole that had burned through the side of the melting train, bringing fire and molten plastic and aluminum with me. I rushed for the escalators leading up to the street above.

"Oh, no you don't!" Mom was hot on my heels.

She was out of the train behind me, and she jumped on top of me as I caught sight of her.

We both rolled over each other, trying to pound each other into the hot ceramic floor. I wasn't sure if it was repeated power shifting or trying to extinguish the flames on us.

Either way, after thirty seconds of bashing and rolling, we managed to put out the flames that were on us.

Both of us were bruised, bleeding, and burned. And the smoke was starting to fill the tunnel.

The knife had fallen out of Mom's holster, and we both rushed for it.

We grabbed it at the same time and fought for control of the weapon.

"Come now, Vasquez; you know you'll live the rest of your life in guilt if you manage to win this."

"So would you!"

"Oh, please. The truth will be recounted by one of both of us anyway."

"Why would you?"

She didn't answer, instead upping her efforts at getting the knife away from me.

I successfully wrenched the knife free from her grasp, cutting a finger in the process. I picked myself up and rushed to the escalators while I still had visual with them. The smoke was becoming thicker, and the tunnel was getting hotter.

Mom lassoed me back and tried to strangle me with the wires she had used to tie me up.

"Maybe you should try calling for help; you were able to do that after the plane crash."

Gripping the knife like I was dangling from a crane, I thrust the knife at her fingers and the wires, struggling to open my air passage.

"You know, I'm the only thing that's keeping you from breathing this smoke."

She was soon struggling against said smoke, and I was able to wrestle myself free.

I reclaimed some of the wires, and made my way up the inactive escalator, keeping the knife pointed at my assailant.

"You think you can escape this quickly? You still have to get by me!"

We both started whipping each other all the way up the escalator.

When we reached the top, she grabbed my hand, and we were once again fighting for possession of the knife, each whipping the other with wires. As the fight for control dragged on, the ever-thickening smoke was enveloping us.

"You can hide, but you can't run, Vasquez Private Eye. Come forth and show yourself."

Mom finally had full control of the knife, but with the smoke, we could only identify each other by our coughing.

Several times, she thrust the knife toward me blindly, each time either missing me or only leaving a minor cut. I was able to utilize this and whip her with the wire.

Pretty soon, we could see each other's silhouettes, and she lunged forward, throwing me against the railing.

"This is it." She coughed for a few seconds. "Any last words before I—*cough*—finish you off for good?"

It was getting hard to breathe, but I still had to say what I wanted. "I regret nothing—*cough*—except that morality is not what it's choked up to be."

She raised the dagger above her head, ready to send it piercing through my flesh like a knight looming over a dying dragon. But before she could bring it down again, I transferred all of my remaining strength into throwing the two of us over the edge.

Within two seconds, we landed on the ceramic floor of the platform. The sound of the impact resonated with the sound of a gushing splat that echoed through the tunnel.

I pitched toward the edge of the platform, stopping just before I toppled over.

I stayed there for maybe two minutes as the smoke took its toll on me.

Pushing myself up to my feet, I was astounded to find that I was still alive. In the blinding smoke, I was just barely able to make out my surroundings.

It wasn't long before I found the sobering entity.

On the baked cement platform, embossed in blood, was the symbol of my triumph.

I could only stare in disbelief. I had never felt emotions toward death until now. The woman who had brought me into this world now laid a ruined mess by her actions and mine.

As a policeman, I had always believed that good would be the victor over evil; the ever-present population of evildoers had convinced me that I would be able to fulfill my desire of an adventurous lifestyle.

Now seeing this woman, the one who gave Alex the gift of sociability, Richard the gift of patience, Shannon the gift of courage, and Zelda the gift of morality, I felt like I was dead.

It was inconceivable that such a person had attempted to kill her only son for cheating death when his brother had not.

I took off the shirt from the fresh facedown corpse and took with me the severed evidence which would undoubtedly prove the case. I wrapped it in the shirt I removed, tied it to my belt loop, and picked up my hat which lay nearby.

As I walked toward where the escalators came down to meet me, I could see the train spitting smoke like I had seen at Wainwright. I remembered the flames from Flight 934, seeing them swelling from the ruined airplane.

The smoke shrouded the flames from view, and I went up the escalator to the street above.

CHAPTER XXVII

The Aftermath

I emerged from the tunnel, gasping for air, and the first thing I saw were police cruisers and fire engines parked on the street. Rachel, Bethany, William, my friends, and a number of my colleagues as well as firemen were waiting for me.

Out of breath, bruised, burned, covered in soot, and cut in several areas, I was such a gruesome sight to look upon.

"Ha!" Rachel pointed a finger at me. She had an eye patch on her left eye. "I caught you red-handed!"

"Yeah, he does have blood on his hands." Alex was still himself despite the fact that it was 10 PM.

"What are you all doing here so quickly?" I was sure that no one would have known where I was, especially during the middle of the night.

"We saw a large smoke plume rising from the tunnel." William had casts on his arms and under his shirt, bandages on and around his head, and a splinted leg; next to me, though, he had hardly a scratch.

"If being slashed and burned three-fifths to death with William in the hospital isn't proof enough for you," I could tell Rachel would refuse to listen to what I was about to say, "then you can give away your uniform to someone who deserves it. I didn't do this to myself, and I can prove to you who it is."

"You always say that; liar, liar, pants on fire."

Alex presented a squirting flower bouquet. "Seriously, your pants are on fire."

I looked down. "So they are."

Alex hosed me down, and I took a few swigs of water while he did that.

After I was put out, Rachel walked up to me, standing between me and the entrance to the tunnel. "So, I see you've managed to kill your last victim, Vasquez Private Eye."

"I'll have you know the 'victim' was the one under the guise of Zachary Venshlin. It was this person who had killed the four men and has sabotaged court cases for the past several years, but they've finally faced justice."

"So, who was it, then?"

I untied the blood-stained shirt from around my waist, reached for the item inside, and gently grabbed the top of the top. "You asked for this, Rachel Jane Dinesen."

With a swift raise of my arm, I removed the shirt like a tarp. Resting in my hand was a severed head covered in burned bruises and charred blood. Soot-imbued blood dripped from the sliced neck, but the head was in better shape than I was. The scorched hair was in a sooty mess around my fingers, but the face, battered and singed as it was, was unmistakable.

I might as well have showed the head of Medusa.

Rachel's face fell apart as she reeled back in shock. Her whole body froze solid. She tried to raise her hand and shield herself from what she was seeing, but her hand would not come in front of her face.

I watched as her visible eye rolled into the back of her head. She took a step back, but she stepped over the edge of the staircase and fell back like a wax sculpture, tumbling into the smoke-filled abyss, her skull fracturing audibly on the ceramic floor below.

I turned around to show the head off to the others. They all gasped in startled fear.

Richard spoke with stopped breath. "Is... that...?"

"Yes. Zachary Jacques Tolono Venshlin, aka Professor Martha Ida Laverne Faulkner-Vasquez."

Shannon screamed and fainted. Zelda took to her heels and ran off. Bethany looked back and forth from the tunnel, to me, to the head in my hand, to William... and fell down to her knees crying.

Alex recovered from his diluted shock. "She must have really lost her head there, huh?"

I affirmed to him, returning the head to the shirt I had picked it out of. "She was after the same person that William was, believe it or not."

William seemed to be confused. "When did I ever say anything of the sort?"

"At the hospital. Remember when you had told us about your role in the crash of Firebird Airlines Flight 934?"

"Oh, yeah. Now I remember."

"She also had a grudge against the passenger who sent the message to air traffic control."

"So, she was the one sabotaging the courts and killing all the people involved in that trial? And it was all because of me taking the blame for Firebird Airlines' failing?"

"Yes. And she knew who it was that ended up costing you your airplane mechanic's license."

"Who was it?"

"That was me."

Everyone turned to look at me in startled surprise.

William looked at the head, and then he looked back at me. He dropped his clutches, collapsed against a lamppost, and threw his head back to look at the clouds. "Is there no mercy left in this world?!"

Richard turned to the smoke plume emanating from the underground tunnel, and then he turned to me. "I think it would be advisory to get to a hospital, Johnson."

With everything that had happened in the last half hour, I agreed. "Yeah, good idea, Richard."

The firemen descended into the tunnel with breathing apparatus, and Shannon and I were taken to the hospital. I can't tell you to this day the elated sensation I had while riding the ambulance.

It was 7:45 AM when the nurse came in. She brought in a tray with my breakfast of oatmeal, applesauce, and milk and set it down in front of me. Alex, Richard, Shannon, and Zelda followed her.

Shannon was wrapped in a blanket and shivering, even though it was 77 degrees in the room. It was obvious she was one fright away from incurable insanity.

My left arm was in a sling, my midsection was wrapped in bandages soaked in burn medicine, and my left leg was cut pretty badly. Apart from that, I was in pretty good condition. The doctors said that I would make a full recovery.

The nurse turned to leave. "If you need anything else, just give me a call."

Once she left, the TV turned up the morning news.

"Police officials have witnessed a dramatic event last night when 27-year-old Officer Johnson Vasquez walked out of a burning subway tunnel carrying the severed head of his 57-year-old mother, Professor Martha Vasquez.

"Ex-Police Chief Bethany Dinesen, who had resigned last night, says that Johnson was investigating a string of court cases which have passed 'not guilty' verdicts to defendants who were truly guilty of the charges pressed against them. Johnson has linked Professor Vasquez as being the mastermind behind the sabotage plot in addition to the serial killing of four men, one of them being her own husband, Detective Daniel Vasquez. Quinn Fichus has the story. Quinn?"

"Thank you, Doreen. Johnson Vasquez and four of his close friends have come to conclude that what started the rampage of Professor Martha Vasquez happened seven years ago today.

"On that day, March 29th, 20—, Firebird Airlines Flight 934 crashed in the Missouri River near Kansas City, Missouri. 75 of the 200 people on board were killed. The cause was deemed by the National Transportation Safety Board to be a maintenance operation that put defective rivets in the plane's vertical fin. The supervisor, 49-year-old William York, was found guilty of willful misconduct, and his mechanic's license was revoked.

"Allegedly, Martha Vasquez enrolled into Wainwright Law Academy under a pseudonym to learn about the justice system. Thirteen trials were rigged with falsified 'not guilty' verdicts over the past five years, and in the last eight months, four men were murdered by Professor Vasquez.

"Vasquez's son, Johnson, and his friends were able to deduce what she was doing, and last night, Johnson was taken hostage by Professor Vasquez. The two engaged in a fiery fight in the subway, and Johnson emerged victorious with Professor Vasquez's severed head.

"When Johnson showed the head to the policemen and firemen gathered outside the subway station last night, Police Chief Dinesen's daughter, Rachel, had reportedly been scared to death upon seeing the head.

"According to testimony from Johnson, Rachel Dinesen had been leading a corrupt investigation into the murders in order to achieve a promotion to police chief. The two officers were in a cutthroat competition to solve the mystery, and when Johnson presented the firm evidence, Rachel was shocked to the point of death.

"Johnson is now under scrutiny from his colleagues about his culpability for Rachel's death, and he is currently at St. Larsson Hospital recovering from his injuries. Now back to Doreen Harper. Doreen?"

I turned off the TV and looked at Zelda. "Any updates about my future?"

"They still haven't been able to come to a consensus on your degree of guilt for Rachel's death, but you might want to look for a backup job just to be safe."

"I'll keep that in mind."

A nurse walked in and presented two envelopes. One was addressed to Zelda, the other for me.

Zelda accepted hers and examined the back side. She saw the sender's name, written on the exterior of the envelope in blood, as Bethany Dinesen. She bit her lip as she carefully opened the envelope.

I looked at the envelope I was given, which also had blood writing on the back of it: "On the 30th of March 20—, this article is to be delivered to the person of Johnson Charlie Clayton Vasquez, NO QUESTIONS ASKED, and in the event of his predecease, *to be destroyed unread.*"

There was no alternative of finding out what would be inside than to tear open the flap which held the paper package shut. I opened it and removed a smaller envelope from within. On the outside, I could see written in turquoise ink florid text; one last poem.

Justice is served; you've seen it first hand
Once you return, it will be your command
Have this story be told to them all

No one will miss out; that's your call
So, do what you must
Out with all your friends
No longer fearing around those bends

Despite the lack of a sender's name, I knew from this message who wrote the letter inside.

Zelda's envelope contained a letter stained with tears and blood. Some of the writing was blood as well. When I opened my envelope, I found a thick stack of folded papers. I unfolded them to read its contents.

Zelda read her letter aloud first, followed by mine.

Chapter XXVIII

Last Will and Testament

When this document reaches mortal eyes, the hand that has scribed these letters will have been put out of its misery. A night's worth of suffering shall never be cured, neither in life nor in afterlife. Even infinite purgatory in hell shall be nothing more than a hornet sting to the ripping out of one's stomach in contrast to the blighted days and nights that have followed the date of March 29th, 20—.

Martha Ida Laverne Faulkner-Vasquez was my elder sister by two years. She was such an ambitiously assiduous woman, and she was always there to help me when I was struggling. She was widely popular with the forensics and chemistry students she taught at Deviltry University, and Shannon Edith Amanda Thomson was one of them.

Never did it cross my mind that Martha would become a serial killer.

I have been forced to accept the punishment for a crime I have not committed. It was a crime that should never have happened; a crime that has left me in ruins for life. Even after I die, I shall remain burdened by this unconscionable act; not even the Devil himself could exceed these tortures. One might believe this to be an exaggeration, but that word is to reality as Graham's number is to a googolplex.

The date was March 29th, 20——. My sister and her sons and husband were returning home from a vacation in Denver, where my ex-husband, Chester Gordon Dinesen, lived with our two sons, Jeffrey and Raymond.

On the evening of the aforementioned date, 187 men, women, and children boarded a Boeing 767 aircraft at Denver International Airport bound for Cincinnati, Ohio as Firebird Airlines Flight 934. The Vasquez family was seated in row 5, a stroll away from the cockpit. The flight was supervised by 11 Firebird Airlines flight attendants, and in the cockpit were the 41-year-old captain, Natasha Lindsay Reynolds and the 38-year-old first officer, Jeremy Walter Bentsen.

The airplane took off from Denver at 8:08 PM, heading east toward Cincinnati. The flight would be due to land after 1:08 AM Eastern Time; as the original arrival time was 11:40 PM, many passengers slept during the climb out of Denver.

The flight would never reach Cincinnati, and a number of the people on board would never again see the light of day. The flight crashed in the Missouri River minutes before 11 PM Central Time.

There were 200 people on the aircraft; by the time the sun arose, 75 were dead, including Terrence Mitchell Vasquez, my youngest nephew. Martha herself lost her left kneecap in the crash.

The National Transportation Safety Board investigated and found the crash to have been caused by a single faulty rivet in the vertical stabilizer.

When the rivet failed, the fin split open, causing the aircraft to go into a slaloming dive toward the city. It careened into a wooded riverbank when the pilots tried to land at a small regional airport.

Though the pilots made the choice to land on a runway that was not designed for a commercial aircraft (especially one that had flight control problems), the flight data recorder and subsequent flight simulator tests showed that they had no hope of reaching Kansas City International Airport in a safe manner.

The airline was sued for malpractice, but through the exclusionary rule, they were acquitted of all charges; instead, accountability for the accident was laid upon the airline's lead mechanic, William Henry Eric York. He was later fired, and an attempt to appeal was unsuccessful, leaving him unemployed.

Unbeknownst to almost everyone involved, this was not the end. In fact, it was only the beginning.

It was years before the first clues surfaced. Trials in the state were reaching controversial verdicts, and the exclusionary rule came under fire from many wary observers. My nephew, Johnson Charlie Clayton Vasquez, has believed that someone was masterminding a plot.

This was confirmed when a series of murders came to light. My daughter, Rachel Jane Dinesen, investigated them on behalf of the police; Johnson investigated the crimes as well in the hopes of avenging the fiery murder of his father, Daniel Jack Vasquez.

Johnson was able to solve this case before Rachel; the murders were connected to the falsified verdicts, and both were an act of revenge for the verdict delivered at the lawsuit trial of Firebird Airlines.

But a spinning twist of fate was yet to come. The killer was my sister, Martha Ida Laverne Vasquez.

Johnson's on-board distress call after the plane crashed lured a fellow police academy student, Zelda Alice Margaret Thomson, to go to Kansas City to investigate the crash. During the course of the investigation, she found that Firebird Airlines was investing in pilot training in favor of aircraft maintenance; their logic was that training pilots to fly dilapidated airplanes would outweigh the need for proper maintenance.

But this evidence was found without a warrant as part of a criminal investigation into Firebird Airlines. And as such, the exclusionary rule gave Firebird Airlines the wiggle room needed to be acquitted of all charges.

This fact was the motive for Martha to kill her son on the seven-year anniversary of his brother's death.

In the scant few hours of last night, seven years to the day after the crash of Firebird Airlines Flight 934, Johnson had been kidnapped by Martha to complete her revenge. A fire was started onboard a subway train, and the two fought each other to the death.

What started as a response to a subway fire would seal the fate of my daughter. Johnson emerged from the tunnel in the presence of me, a number of my officers, firefighters, and Johnson's friends. He was covered in soot, burns, bruises, and cuts, but all of that paled in comparison to what he presented to his compatriots.

As though he were Perseus, Johnson presented Rachel a glimpse of my sister's severed head. The mere sight of it was enough to instill death unto her.

And after she collapsed into the tunnel, Johnson turned around to show us all the killer's identity. It sounds nothing to hear, but it was hellish to see.

It was tedious to recount these events, but I assure you that there exists no simpler way to explain the circumstances of my suffering.

Johnson has infested his conscience with an irreparable bloodstain with the deaths of two of his blood relatives. I shall never know if he is, in fact, responsible for the death of his father, the judge, and the two lawyers; but as the court ruling which had metastasized into a meticulous serial murder came about because he was the one to make the post-crash distress call on Firebird Airlines Flight 934, I have reason to believe this may well be the case.

And he has left me to burn by every possible course of action to take in response to the death of my daughter.

Revenge has long been the most primary of all human impulses. One longs to wreak a wrong upon another that the other has committed against them or someone close to them. It's an involuntary impulse to exact revenge, and Martha had done just that when Firebird Airlines was acquitted. That has left me with the conclusion that revenge shall cause ill results to take shape.

When someone brings about the death of a coworker, their boss must send them away and have them arrested. But in the case of William Henry Eric York, he had been established as the source of Martha's murder spree; he was fired from his job as an airplane mechanic after being blamed for the crash of Flight 934, and he had also committed murder because of the court ruling; it would consequently be unacceptable for me to fire Johnson, as he would be prone to kill his future wife.

Suicide could, in theory, put an end to all suffering. Far from correct, it's the opposite that proves true. William had at one point attempted suicide, but he is still alive and has been talked out of trying to kill himself. And even after my mortal life is over, I cannot guarantee that my spirit shall not retain the memories it had before death, or even that I shall be born into a new life.

How, then, shall I relieve myself of this torture?

I cannot remain here, knowing that I have been nailed to the wall and left for dead. I must therefore step down from the position of Police Chief and seek asylum in France. There, I can remain isolated from the inescapable truth that everyone houses a dark and sinister lust for torture.

Knowing I can never return to the United States after I leave, I, Bethany Teresa Dinesen, being of as sound mind and body as I shall ever hope to be in what remains of my life, do make this document my last will and testament.

At the moment at which I take my leave, be it from the United States by physical means or from the world by spiritual means, I do bequeath all of my worldly possessions as follows:

Unto the senior detective of the Police Department of Cincinnati, Zelda Alice Margaret Thomson, I leave to succeed me as Police Chief.

Unto my ex-husband, Chester Gordon Dinesen, I leave the funds and accounts which are currently held in my name.

Unto my two sons, Jeffrey Peter Dinesen and Raymond Albert Dinesen, I shall leave my former estate in Cincinnati.

And lastly, unto my nephew, Johnson Charlie Clayton Vasquez, I shall leave but a word of caution: The Fates shall in good time complete the execution your mother has not.

Chapter XXIX

The Killer's Story

My Wayward Son:

If you are reading this article, it means that you have succeeded in fulfilling your lifelong dream. I have understood how close you have been to your father, and as of recently, your rivalry with Rachel.

I cannot prefigure what you will think of me by the time this document is opened to you, whether as a madwoman, a psychopath, or even a cold-hearted devil.

What I want you to understand is that while I did mean to execute an elaborate operation of vengeance unto those who lay at fault for allowing the death of your younger brother to go unreciprocated, I wanted the lone surviving member of the new Vasquez generation to lead a happy life. (Since you're reading this, it means you have no need to die at this age.)

Since I have not thoroughly expounded my preparations for committing these crimes, I have chosen to unveil all that I dare to write about in relation to the thoughts and events that have weighed upon me.

For the past seven years, I have been subjected to an ever-crushing insanity after the crash of Firebird Airlines Flight 934, which resulted in the loss of my left kneecap as well as your brother, Terrence Mitchell Vasquez.

And the "not guilty" verdict at the lawsuit trial made any hope of mental recovery unattainable, especially since it was you who provided the evidence which convicted William York at the trial.

I started engaging in highly debauched activities such as drinking, smoking, and gambling. From there, I became less and less the woman I once was. My spending went haywire and I started searching for any money I could find. Even now, I'm amazed that I was able to keep it secret.

It was during October 20— when I heard the call from The Fates for what I should do.

The date was Friday, August 22, 20—. It had been six months since my mental stability had disintegrated. I was in desperate need of money to support my newfound addictions to gambling, smoking, and drinking. My intention was to break into Dr. Chuckle's Prank Lab and Gag Shop and replenish my supply of money.

Knowing the risk of stealing from your friend, I had to enlist an accomplice to get the dough. And after 10 PM, he got himself in the store to steal the money while I hid in the alley adjacent to the store.

What I saw next was truly shocking. My hit man came running out of the store and down the street, followed by what I thought was a secret agent.

Ten minutes later, the police arrived. I realized they had been alerted to the alarm that sounded when the agent smashed through the window, and I hid in a dumpster, looking through a hole that had rusted through the side.

Another ten minutes passed, and I saw my man being held at gunpoint by the secret agent, who was coercing him to the store where the police were waiting.

The would-be robber was arrested, and the mysterious agent was questioned by one of the officers. The man revealed himself as Brandon Chide, and he claimed that he was hired by Alex to guard his store.

I remembered that Alex's business name was "Franklin Chuckle", and I realized something.

"Dr. Chuckle and Mr. Chide" seemed melodious with another well-known pair; this screamed a dark force (beyond me) at work, and I had to find out what it was.

Over the next few weeks, I monitored the shop to see what was going on there.

I saw that Chide had wired a police scanner to the shop and was chasing down criminals every night; criminals whom I recognized as being on the most wanted list.

But every time daytime came around, there was no sign of Chide anywhere.

One night, I slipped into the store while Chide was out pursuing another man to investigate the basement. I had been to the shop many times since my first sighting of Chide, but not the basement.

I discovered evidence that someone had been working at the drink station with chemicals that were not something you would normally see. I took notes of what those chemicals were, hoping I would be able to exploit it for my own gain.

When Chide returned to the basement, I hid behind the drink station. It was 6 AM, and I was able to watch a spectacle that confirmed my healthy suspicions about "Dr. Chuckle" and "Mr. Chide".

I realized that my young student, Shannon Thomson, was the only person with the experience needed to create these potions. I started sending her the chemicals which were needed for the elixirs, which I planned to use for my own gain.

I had her bring the finished product to an alley behind Wainwright Law Academy, where I could obtain the goods in a clandestine manner. Shannon would not have had the courage to tell the police about this.

When I tested the potions on myself, I found myself to be a completely new being; a man with a magnified thirst for justice. He would impose a horrifying revenge upon those who shattered the delicate sanity of his original form.

My name choice of Zachary Jacques Tolono Venshlin was the first in a series of inklings of my intentions.

I enrolled into Wainwright Law Academy as Zachary Venshlin so as to better understand my enemy: the law. During my four years of dedicated study, I started formulating and creating the necessary elements of my rampage. I wrote poems to mock you as well as provide clues to foreshadow each of the murders.

This document was written during the time you were at the hospital after William tried to kill himself outside Rachel's apartment, and completed just after I'd sedated you.

I was ashamed that my sister, Bethany, had such a brat for a daughter as Rachel. I knew her secrets before you found out after the death of your father. I had planned to exploit her character flaws of greed and pride to lure her away from the real truth through the notes I left for you. I wanted this to be solved by you and your friends.

You can probably figure out how I was able to kill each of the four men involved, but it might be satiating to know how you were subdued and taken on the train.

As you've probably suspected, I did indeed summon you and your friends to my house intent on taking you hostage. I simply had to sedate you long enough to get you on the subway train.

I didn't want your death to be poisoning by the sedative I planned to administer; that kind of death would be too lenient. What's more, I would never have been able to know if you did manage to solve the mystery.

What I did was I dissolved 10 sleeping pills in a glass of water and marinated a set of silverware in the solution. Then as I set the table, I gave you the drugged silverware while I set the other spots with clean silverware.

This technique would allow sedation without affecting the other four people that were present at the table or attracting suspicion from any of you five.

Even though you were the root cause of everything you had witnessed in the last seven years, I felt it unjust to kill you before you achieved something meaningful in your life.

I would have accepted the outcome of our confrontation regardless of who escaped alive.

If it was me, I would've completed my revenge plot and been able to expose the truth of the world to all.

If it were you, you would've done the same thing, but my death would cause controversy within your work place and call into question the noble purpose of its existence.

Clearly, because of the fact that you're reading this, the outcome was that of the latter.

I have sought to convince the world that true evildoers are the rulers of society that express greed and selfish lust unto the insects that reside across the planet; they are the reason good people are made bad. But even in the face of burning evidence to incriminate them, very few people are at all willing to accept this truth.

William York, I, and quite possibly you have expressed victimization of crime by committing wrong. But no one would stand against Firebird Airlines for being the root cause of my, your, or William's behavior.

The reason for this blind denial is this:

Evil is like death; the truth lies beyond what the mortal eye can see, and only those who have been consumed by it can know what dreadful secrets hide under its disguise.

What you have read can very well let you understand the kinds of torture the world goes through. You can either find a way to correct this problem or find a way to escape it.

I want you to tell the world about your experience of my fanatical rage so that such a sequence can never take shape again. Crucially, I want the world to accept the fact that crime is not limited to the choices made by the criminal, but is a side effect of what takes place in view of the world's blind eye.

Do what it right, Johnson. I may be dead, but I can still get my ends met. Only you can expose the character flaws of the oblivious world.

From beyond the grave,

Professor Martha Ida Laverne Vasquez née Faulkner

Chapter XXX

The Endgame

I spent about a week in the hospital recovering from my injuries. Two people stopped in to visit me during my stay. It took a moment, but I was able to recognize the pair as Natasha Reynolds and Jeremy Bentsen, the pilots of Firebird Airlines Flight 934.

"Can you believe what had happened Sunday night?"

"I don't know which is crazier; the plane crash we went through or the serial murders that happened in the last year."

Natasha pulled up a seat for her and Jeremy.

"What are you two doing here?"

"We saw the news reports on Monday about the fire in the subway, and we thought we'd stop by."

"Yeah. I can't believe anyone would commit these acts because of a plane crash."

"Have you heard about the Überlingen mid-air collision in 2002?"

"Right. Of course, only one murder was committed as a result of that, not five."

"You're still alive, and the doctors say you'll recover."

"I meant William York killing his father."

"Ah, I see."

"It's like I always told my friends: money can end lives, money can distort the truth, and money can give people a false sense of satisfaction."

"Which is why we had both stopped flying for Firebird Airlines after the crash of Flight 934."

"Thanks for getting us out of there, by the way."

"You're welcome. So, what are you two doing now?"

"We fly for a different airline now, which we know has much more concern with safety over profit."

"What airline is that?"

"We're flying for World Travelling Flyers."

"They're the guys that operate flights going all the way around the world, right?"

"With stopovers on the way, yes."

"How's that working for you?"

"It's all good. I can say they're a model airline."

"I'm glad you two are enjoying it."

"So, how have you been holding up?"

"Well, I can certainly say that I'm grateful that I'm here to talk to someone; though it's a surprise that that someone is the pilots of the flight that started this whole debacle."

"Yeah, it's not every day that that happens."

"No, it's not."

"Have you heard anything about William York? It's my understanding that the two of you had worked together at one point in time."

"We did. The last I saw of him was just before I got in the ambulance to be taken to the hospital."

"What happened then?"

"I had told him that I had sent a distress message to air traffic control after the crash, which ended up passing the buck to William instead of Firebird Airlines."

"He probably didn't take it too well, did he?"

"He was devastated that the man who helped clear him of accountability for the murders was the one who caused all of his initial troubles."

"It's like Firebird's logic of training pilots to fly planes with major problems instead of maintaining its fleet."

"They did get away with it for a long time, and even after the crash, they still insisted that we wouldn't have been able to save any lives if they hadn't trained us for that kind of emergency."

"That report about Firebird's maintenance pretty much threw them out of law's reach."

"I heard that Firebird's CEO, Nicholas Althorn, is being questioned about the murders that have taken place."

"He is. Jeremy and I were among the people who were at the hearings."

"I wonder how he reacted to the pilots of the airline's worst accident being there to watch him get grilled."

"He was startled, that's for sure."

"I'm sure he was."

"Yeah. He gave us a message when we met with him: *It's been seven years since 75 people died in the crash of Flight 934, and only now do I realize the full scope of the tragedy. I could not have predicted the subsequent murders committed as a consequence of dodging justice, but I now know from a crash survivor's testimony that in pursuit of evasion of justice, they nearly paid their life for saving the lives of Natasha Reynolds and Jeremy Bentsen.*

I do apologize to Mr. Johnson Vasquez for the loss of his brother, Terrence Vasquez, and their mother's brash and wrathful acts of murder. I also want William York to know that we wish to do whatever is necessary to help him recover from the injustice invoked upon him by this company. I am aware that there is damage done which is likely beyond recovery, seeing as five acts of murder have been committed, as well as two attempts at murder and one other death.

Let this be a lesson to all corporations the world over: there can be nothing good that will come out of cheating your way out of justice when you've committed wrong against many innocent people. The bad luck brought by a broken mirror only lasts seven years, and at the end of those seven years, the fuller consequences will emerge.

Sincerely,

Nicholas Ronald Althorn, ex-Chief Executive Overseer of Firebird Airlines, Inc."

"I should hope the message is heeded."

"Me, too."

"Well, we should probably get going; we need to be in Boston by tomorrow morning. Here are our numbers."

"Okay, thanks." I gave the pilots my number as well.

"We'll see you when we get back."

"Bye, Jeremy. Bye, Natasha."

"Bye, Johnson."

And with that, they were out the door and gone.

My story has drawn to a close, and at the final request of the late Martha Vasquez, I have published the account of my four friends and me of the investigation into the murders of six people whose fate was sealed seven years in the past.

I still vividly remember that day, seven years later.

Alex's still worked at Dr. Chuckle's Prank Lab and Gag Shop, and he continued his adventures as Brandon Chide. Until now, his secret had gone untold outside the ring of us five.

Richard went on to be a Major League Baseball player, and Shannon was admitted into a psychiatric hospital. She was released after two years of treatment, and the two got married afterward.

Zelda still is haunted by the sight of me carrying my mom's severed head. Despite this, she and I were married eight weeks after Mom's death. We are now living peacefully with two children and a third on the way.

Firebird Airlines went out of business after they finally accepted full responsibility for the crash of Flight 934; the fact that six people were killed as a consequence of their acquittal sent Nicholas Althorn on a very long guilt trip.

The last anyone heard from the airline was paying out all of its assets amongst the families of each of the 200 people that were aboard Flight 934 and to William York.

William was able to return to the working society after receiving compensation from Firebird Airlines. He decided not to go back to being an airplane mechanic, instead working as a construction worker building houses.

As for me, I learned a very important lesson. There are always consequences for everything in life, and no matter how far away you think you are from them, they will come back and take you by surprise.

After my recovery, I resigned from my job in the police force. Mom's attempt on my life was enough of an impetus for me to leave, and even though Zelda was the police chief, I was skeptical about not being fired. But I still felt that being in the police force was the biggest mistake of my life.

Ever since then, I've been unable to decide if what I did on Firebird Airlines Flight 934 had saved lives or sealed fates. Or if I did both, did I do more of one than the other? All I do know is that it opened my eyes to the real world.

I did feel a bit sore about myself seeing that I had been a mindless drone for an organization that beats down on people who were the victim of their own lives instead of making their own choice. Mom and William had opened my eyes to the fact that labelling people as criminals was simply a hollow excuse for the police to exercise despotic control over other people.

As a consequence, it was clear that my message had to be sent through to the world. I know there will be many that won't focus on the real message and instead think about ways to suppress those who are unfortunate enough to be frowned on by society.

But as long as the police beats down on society for its imperfections, there will always be someone who knows their dirty secrets.

I suppose that Mom was happy in a way since Firebird Airlines has fallen to the history books. Even though she paid a hefty price for making it happen, thousands of other people are now happy that Firebird Airlines has at long last been properly dealt with.

I mounted her head on my bedroom wall as a reminder of the painful lessons that had come out of the spree, and it still stands there today.